BAD KARMA

A Zoey Callaway Mystery

DEBI CHESTNUT

BAD KARMA

Copyright © 2020 by Debra Chestnut
www.AuthorDebiChestnut.com

This book is a work of fiction. Names, characters, places, and incidents are the product of the author's imagination or are used fictitiously. Any resemblance to actual events, locales, or persons, living or dead, is coincidental.

All rights reserved. No part of this publication may be reproduced, distributed, or transmitted in any form or by any means, including photocopying, recording, or other electronic or mechanical methods, without the prior written permission of the publisher, except in the case of brief quotations embodied in critical reviews and certain other noncommercial uses permitted by copyright law.

For permission requests, contact publisher below:

Cayélle Publishing/Monocle Imprint
Lancaster, California USA
www.CayellePublishing.com

Orders by U.S. trade bookstores and wholesalers, please contact Freadom Distribution: Tel: (833) 229-3553 ext 813 or email Freadom@Cayelle.com

Cover Art by Robin Ludwig Design, Inc.
Interior Design & Typesetting by Ampersand Book Interiors
Printed in the United States of America
ISBN: 978-1-952404-13-9 [paperback]
ISBN: 978-1-952404-14-6 [ebook]
Library of Congress Control Number 2020940414

DEDICATION

I dedicate this book to my writing mentor, James Parsons. This book wouldn't have been possible without your valuable input and assistance. To my husband, Lonnie, who has always encouraged me to follow my dreams.

CHAPTER ONE

It wasn't even nine a.m. and I was already having a bad day. I was working on Project Shadow for the FBI. Suspected human traffickers. I shook my head. What some people won't do for money! The FBI occasionally hires a freelance information professional like me to dig into the lives of "persons of interest" as they call it, when they need to circumvent the law – and they pay extremely well.

Anyway, the database I needed to complete the project was down and my call to tech support was a waste of time. I wound up talking to some guy on the other side of the planet named Pardeep. He was pleasant enough, and his English quite intelligible. He tried to help, but in the end he couldn't fix the problem, leaving me behind the eight-ball with the FBI. With nothing left to do but wait, I decided to go for a run.

A wall of cool air hit me as I stepped out the door of my apartment; rain-laden clouds darkened the western sky. Thunder rumbled in the distance as I popped my earbuds in and hit my favorite playlist. With luck, I'd be able to complete my five miles and be back home before the early fall storm hit.

I was just hitting my stride, listening to Aerosmith doing "Walk this Way," one of my favorites, when the phone call came. Damn it, I had told Pardeep not to call for another hour. I guess hours pass quicker in India. I stopped running and gulped in air as I wheezed a weak, "Hello."

"Is this Zoey Callaway?" The voice was not Pardeep's. This voice was low, sultry, and very sexy. He sounded hot, I thought, but he's probably short, fat and bald, so don't get too excited, Zoe.

"Yes," I said between breaths. I willed my heart rate to lower itself. "Who is this?"

"Miss Callaway, my name is Seth Andrews. I'm a detective with the Hope Harbor Police Department."

My stomach flipped. The detective continued. "I'm sorry to have to do this over the phone, but I'm afraid I have some bad news. I believe Felix Callaway is your uncle. Is that correct?"

My mouth dried up. I couldn't talk. I managed to squeak a response, "Yes, he's my uncle...why? What—?"

"I'm truly sorry," the voice cut in. "A neighbor found your uncle this morning. I'm afraid he's dead."

My legs turned to rubber. Oh God, not Felix. Not Uncle Felix. Dropping to my knees, I managed to sit myself down on a lawn next to the sidewalk.

"What do you mean he's dead? I saw him a few days ago. He can't be dead." This was not happening. No, no, no! Not Uncle Felix. He couldn't die. We had so much to do.

"I'm sorry, Miss Callaway. I wish I didn't have to make this call. I'd rather we talk in person. Yours was the only number we could find. We still need to talk to you, however, and it should be face-to-face. Are you able to come to the station?"

And then the tears came, cascading down my face, soaking my cheeks and entering the corners of my half-open mouth I tasted the salt and looked through unseeing eyes at the empty street before me.

I could still picture Felix at his desk. Pictures, notes, and newspaper clippings littered the large whiteboard in his office, all connected by thin pieces of red string. He called it organized chaos; I called it a mystery and I'd loved every minute of trying to figure it out. There'd be no more of that, no more sitting at the kitchen table rehashing old cold cases he'd worked on at the sheriff's office. No more bear hugs and encouraging words… somewhere in the distance a voice was calling.

"Hello, Miss Callaway, are you still there?"

"Ye-yes, I'm here detective. I'm two hours away, I'll get there as soon as I can. Thank you."

"That's fine. When you get to the station, just tell the front desk you're there to see me. Do you know where the police station is?"

"Yes, I do. Thanks." I tapped my phone to end the call.

I don't know how long I sat on the grass. No one stopped to help me. It's just as well; I would have probably snapped their head off if they had. I walked back to my apartment in the pouring rain. There was no run left in me. My energy was spent, and all I wanted to do was crawl into bed and forget this day ever happened.

I climbed the stairs to my front door, and with shaking hands managed to get the key into the lock.

My apartment is small. In fact, calling it an apartment would do nothing but massage my mom's ego. It's little more than a glorified attic over my mom's garage. Still, it has all the amenities; a convenience kitchen where you can sit on the couch, watch TV, and cook dinner all without ever getting up; a bathroom with a shower and toilet that works if you reach into the water tank and flip the mechanism to flush. The handle broke a year ago. She may be my mom, but she's a lousy landlord. I finished my shower, packed a suitcase, and my laptop.

It hit me as I was about to get in the car and saw Mom's car right beside mine.

"Damn! I need to tell her," I said to the open door. "Well, isn't this going to be peachy."

You know how some people can brighten a room just by walking into it? It's not that way with my mother. She could start a fight in an empty room. I know, I've seen her do it.

I tossed my bags into my Jeep and walked to the side door of my Mom's house.

Walking into my mother's kitchen was like time travel. Every time I set foot in there it was like being in a seventy's sitcom, complete with puke green appliances, harvest gold countertops, and dark cupboards. Mom calls it vintage; I have a few other words for it – none of which can be uttered in mixed company.

She was standing at the counter chopping vegetables for a salad.

"Zoey, what are you doing here?" Mom said. She glanced up giving me the once over, her eyes bloodshot as usual. "Aren't you supposed to be working?"

"I work from home, or have you forgotten?"

She raised her eyebrows. "When are you going to get a real job?"

The tears were back, and I was having a hard time standing again. "I need to sit. You should sit too," I said and plopped down in a chair at the dinette set.

She wiped her hands on a towel and sat across the table from me. Her hair – it was blond this week – fell in front of her eyes.

She brushed it aside with the back of her hand and said, "What is it? What's so bad you're all in tears?"

"There's no easy way to say this. Uncle Felix is dead." I locked eyes with her, but she turned away. I could see it hadn't quite registered. It took a moment and then she turned back to face me.

"How…how do you know this?"

"The police called me. They found his body this morning. I have to go to Hope Harbor. They need me to come in."

"They called you? Why? I'm his sister for God's sake, why call you?" Her brow furrowed, and her eyes became slits.

I could sense the resentment in her. She wasn't upset about Felix—she was pissed that I was the one they called.

"I'm sorry, Mom, I have to go. I'll call when I know more." A tear ran down her cheek, and the hurt radiated out of her eyes. For a moment, I felt sorry for her. She hadn't had an easy life, but then, a lot of her troubles were her own doing.

"Do what you need to do. Just don't make the funeral for Saturday. I have plans. Friday would be better."

I resisted the sudden urge to pour myself a large glass of wine, but I had a long drive ahead of me. Mom rose from the table and went back to chopping her vegetables. "Drive safely."

I nodded and escaped through the back door. Enough damage had been done for one day.

Before leaving, I checked my mail. There was a package wrapped in an old brown grocery bag. it was from Felix. "What the hell?" I said and set the box down on the passenger seat. As much as I was dying to open it, I knew I couldn't afford to get sidetracked.

On the way to Hope Harbor I kept casting a sideways glance at the package. It just didn't make sense. We saw each other two or three times a month, why didn't he just give this to me when

I was there over the weekend? My stomach lurched. Was Felix sick and hadn't told me?

Traffic was light, and I made it to Hope Harbor by noon and decided to drive by Uncle Felix's house on the way to the police station.

His Craftsman style house sat on Ashley Lane and was within walking distance of downtown. Old oak trees shaded the front porch and yard, and there was plenty of space between houses for privacy, if there was such a thing in Hope Harbor. It was a small town where secrets were hard to keep. I'd spent enough time here over the years to get to know a lot of people and Hope Harbor felt like home.

The house was surrounded by police and emergency vehicles, so I parked on the street and made my way up the porch steps toward the front door. A policeman stopped me as I approached and told me to wait outside while he got Detective Andrews.

As I waited, I could see the neighbors rubbernecking, wondering what was happening. No doubt the whole town knew by now and I could feel my face flush as I considered the stories they must be telling about what happened to Felix. I made for the door, keeping an eye on the neighbors. I ran smack dab into a broad-chested man about a foot taller than me.

"Where do you think you're going?" he said. It was the voice from the phone.

"I want to see my uncle," I said, meeting his steely gaze with my own.

"Ah, you must be Miss Callaway." His eyes softened. "I'm Detective Seth Andrews. I'm sorry, that's just not possible right now; the crime techs are processing the scene. Here, let's go into the kitchen where we will be out of the way."

We threaded our way into the kitchen through a gaggle of policemen and crime techs. Seth pulled a chair out for me and motioned for me to sit. The detective sat in the chair next to mine.

"I thought you were going to meet me at the police station," he said, his eyes narrowing.

"Good thing I don't always follow directions, because you're obviously not there," I said. "Can you please tell me what happened?"

I looped the strap of my purse over the back of the chair and rested my arms on the worn farm table with my hands folded.

"A neighbor, Mister Lewis, came over to check on your uncle this morning. They were supposed to meet at Gil's Diner for breakfast, but your uncle never showed up. He found your uncle in the bathtub, dead. Mister Lewis called the police, and when I got here, he gave me your phone number. There's no sign of foul play, but all deaths are investigated."

"I don't understand. I just saw him this past weekend. He was fine," I said.

"You saw him this past weekend?" He leaned forward, the muscles in his face clenched.

"Yes," I said. "We hung out, watched TV, went to dinner, and talked. Did he have a heart attack?"

"We won't know for sure until after the autopsy, but there weren't any obvious signs. He looked peaceful. Did you get any indication that he was depressed or upset? There was a bottle of sleeping pills on the vanity."

"No, nothing," I said after a moment of thought. Uncle Felix did seem a little preoccupied, but nothing that raised any alarms. "Uncle Felix took one pill a night before he went to bed. He was very careful with all his medication. If you think my uncle committed suicide, you're barking up the wrong tree." I turned away from the detective; my eyes filled with tears.

"Where are you staying so we can keep in touch?" He pulled a handkerchief out of his suit coat pocket and handed it to me.

"Thank you. I'm staying here," I said, wiping my eyes. The smell of his cologne on the hanky somehow made me feel warm and safe. It was a familiar scent, but I couldn't put my finger on it.

"It's going to be another couple of hours before we're out of here," he said. "Have you got a place you can go in the meantime? I expect the coroner will release your uncle's body tomorrow or the next day. You might want to make arrangements."

"Thanks." I got up from my chair and grabbed my purse. I tried to return his handkerchief, but he waved me off.

"Here's my card," he said. "Call me if you need anything."

I nodded and tucked the card into my purse before making my way out to my car. The butterflies in my stomach wouldn't stop fluttering. I felt lightheaded, I was cold all over, and I had a headache.

It was after four by the time I'd finished finalizing the funeral arrangements. I called Mom on the way back to Felix's house to fill her in on today's activities.

I drove back to Felix's house and pulled into the driveway. Thankfully, all the police personnel were gone. I let myself in and looked around the living room. At least they hadn't made a big mess for me to clean up.

Karma, the black kitten Uncle Felix had adopted a couple of weeks ago, greeted me at the door. In all the excitement, I'd completely forgotten about her. She rubbed her tiny body against my legs as her mournful squeaky mews protested the day's events.

"You poor thing," I said, scooping the squirming fluff of black fur up in my arms, "you must be starving."

I took her into the kitchen and filled her food and water bowls. After she'd eaten, I saw that she had disappeared again. She was clearly distressed by all the activity.

I walked back into the living room and saw Felix's recliner sitting by the window. The blanket he used to cover his legs was unfolded and in the seat. His glasses still sat on the end table, along with a pencil and a newspaper turned to the crossword puzzle.

As I walked down the hallway to look for Karma, I paused outside the bathroom door. I willed myself to cross the threshold. My heart was racing, and my palms were sweating. I stepped just inside the door and saw that the sleeping pills the detective had said were on the bathroom vanity were now gone. Must have taken them for evidence. A fine layer of fingerprint powder covered almost every surface.

I looked over at the bathtub and saw that it was still wet and soiled. As I stood staring at the bathtub, it dawned on me, Felix never took baths. He hated them. He much preferred a hot shower. What the hell?

My stomach heaved. Clamping my hand over my mouth, I bolted for the kitchen sink just in time to see my breakfast for a second time today. I washed my face and hands and continued to walk through the house.

When I opened the door to Felix's office, I froze. Felix and I had spent hours in this room over the years trying to solve some cold cases he'd left behind when he retired from the sheriff's department. Growing up, I had spent countless days with Felix, because my mother was out gallivanting around with the man of the moment.

We would go fishing off the pier in the park. Sometimes I'd play in the playground while he fished, but I wasn't out of his sight for a second – he guarded me like a hawk. After fishing, we would go to lunch and laugh and talk for hours.

When I got older, Felix introduced me to the world of crime. Not committing them, solving them. I was hooked. I wanted to be a cop and follow in his footsteps in the worst way. There was just one problem – I've been terrified of guns ever since my father accidently killed himself while he was cleaning his rifle.

And now the room was empty. The large whiteboard, normally filled with photos, index cards, and notes, was empty, and his laptop was missing.

The floor to ceiling bookshelves that housed the prized collection of first edition books we'd been collecting for years had been rifled through. We'd organized the collection by author, and I quickly scanned the shelves. It looked as though all the books were there.

All that remained was his desk and chair and the worn chintz easy chair I would sit in when we were working. The drawers of the desk had been dumped on the hardwood floor - the contents scattered across the boards. The printer sat on the desk, its cords dangling. I checked his file cabinet and discovered the file on the cold cases was nowhere to be found.

Oh my God, had someone broken in? No, Detective Andrews would have mentioned it to me. But there was no reason the police would have taken anything. Maybe someone came into the house after the police had left.

CHAPTER TWO

I bolted from the office and into the kitchen to retrieve my cell phone, Karma hot on my heels. I had questions that needed answers and Detective Andrews was going to provide them, whether he wanted to or not.

I grabbed my purse, fished out his card, and punched the numbers into my cell phone. My gut twisted in knots, my heart pounded and every muscle in my body tensed. How dare they take anything from Felix's house!

After what felt like an eternity, he picked up my call.

"Detective Andrews," he said. "Can I help you?"

"Yes," I said through clenched teeth. "You can tell me what the hell happened to my uncle's stuff?" I paced around the table, fighting the urge to kick something.

"Ah, Miss Callaway! I don't understand. Is something wrong?"

"Yes, there's something wrong." And he knows it, the pompous ass. "Someone ransacked my uncle's office and removed his personal property. Do you know about this?"

"Yes, we removed some items from the home," he said. "Normal procedure."

Normal procedure, my ass.

"Really?" Now all I wanted to do was slap him. "Why is that?"

"We're trying to determine whether your uncle's death was accidental, natural causes, or a suicide. The items we removed might lead us to a conclusion. I assure you, it's all above board," he said.

I thought about the missing files that'd been in the top drawer of the file cabinet. "So, you go through a man's personal belongings and take what you want without permission?"

"We're looking into your uncle's death, just like we would with any other person who dies at home. It also appears your uncle may have been involved in a matter currently under investigation by the police department, and we're trying to determine if it's connected to his death," he said.

"But you're calling it an accidental death, right? So how does it follow that you needed to take his personal stuff out of the house?" I had to sit. This was going nowhere fast, and he was on my last nerve.

"I'm sorry, Miss Callaway, I have to go. I have a meeting."

The line went dead, but my phone didn't disconnect and, just as I was about to hang up, I heard a series of clicks.

"Ugh!" I screamed. I hurried back to Felix's office and pulled out the remaining folders from the file cabinet. I remembered him showing me a file that contained his life insurance policy when I was there visiting a few months ago.

The stark white board and bare desk made me feel uneasy, as I was used to the chaos of papers, diagrams, and items being taped to just about any available surface. My hands were shaking and my whole body felt like it was vibrating. I replaced the drawers in the desk, but couldn't make myself sit in Felix's chair, so I grabbed the easy chair and settled myself in and got to work.

I managed to find a life insurance policy, and a file that contained a piece of paper with company names and what I assumed were passwords to the online accounts he used to pay bills, and a couple of CDs labeled, "recovery" that'd been hidden behind one of the drawers.

I dashed out to my Jeep to retrieve my laptop; when I opened the car door, I saw the package Felix had sent me laying on the front seat. Damn, I'd forgotten all about it.

After depositing my laptop on the couch, I sat down at the kitchen table and opened the package. It was a book. On the dust jacket was a sticky note in Felix's handwriting that said, "Find what's inside."

At first glance, other than being a modern first edition, the book wasn't rare or collectible. I turned the pages one by one looking for any mark or note in the margins. After finding nothing, I tossed the book on the table.

"What am I missing?" I said, eyeing the book. "Find what's inside. Hmm, maybe…"

I picked up the book and, upon examining it, noticed a slight gap between the spine and the boards that shouldn't be present in a new book.

After rummaging around in the kitchen drawers, I found a thin wooden shish kabob skewer and eased it into the top of the gap. A few agonizing seconds later, there was a clunk as something dropped onto the kitchen table. A flash drive had fallen out of the spine.

"Gotcha!"

I grabbed my laptop and placed it on the table. I inserted the flash drive, and a window appeared. There was a folder marked "Research" and a file named "List."

I selected the list file and three names appeared together on the screen: Chloe Manning, Jenny Parker, Lisa Conrad. On a separate line was the name Lacey Daniels and the words "con-nected to the others?"

Lacey Daniels? I knew her; she was from Hope Harbor. Her father was an attorney and supplied me with work on a regular basis. I'd talked to her a few times when I dropped work off at her father's office. What was this about? What about the other girls? Why didn't Felix tell me about this last weekend?

I tried to open the research folder, but it was password pro-tected. I tried everything; every word I could think of that related to Felix including the passwords from his office. Nothing worked.

When I did a search on Lacey, I found she'd run away two weeks ago. Really? Lacey? She was an honor student and worked in her father's office after school. She didn't seem the type, but one never knows what goes on behind closed doors.

I could understand why Felix wanted to find her, but what was so important that he hid the information in a book spine with a password-protected file? And since when had he started working on active cases? There had to be more to this.

I ran another search and found a few newspaper articles and taped news feeds. I watched a couple of videos of news confer-ences of Chloe's mother begging her to come home. I recog-nized one of the men in the background. He was my contact at the FBI. We'd meet to exchange information because he didn't want to leave an email trail. Yet there'd been no mention of the FBI being involved in anything I'd read … and why would the FBI be involved with a runaway?

None of this made any sense. I got up and made a pot of coffee. Karma, who'd worked her way onto the kitchen table, sat watching me.

"What we have here," I said to her, "is a total lack of information."

She mewed her response.

I took my laptop off the kitchen table and set it up in Felix's office.

Being an information professional allowed me access, for a hefty price, to databases that contain a wealth of information, if you know how to find it. I use the databases and other resources to gather information for my clients and put it all together in a report.

Just after I'd logged in, I heard a voice call out from the living room. Hadn't I locked the front door?

I walked into the living room to see that Felix's next-door neighbor Abby, a casual friend of mine, had let herself in. She rushed towards me and threw her long, lanky arms around me, pulling me close and hugging me to the point I couldn't breathe. Her scarecrow frame pressed into me, and her wiry blond hair washed over my face as she held me. I extricated myself from her embrace and invited her to sit.

"Poor Felix. Was it his heart? Are you okay?" Abby said. She led me into the kitchen and put me in a chair. She poured coffee for each of us and sat down opposite me.

I took a sip of coffee, "No, it wasn't his heart. How was Felix the last few days? Did you see him?"

Abby stared into her coffee cup. "He seemed a little preoccupied, a tad off center. You know how he gets moody sometimes, Hun."

"Did he say what was bothering him?"

"Not really." She got up and washed out her cup in the sink. "I have to get home and start dinner. When's the funeral?"

"Friday at ten," I said. "Christie's Funeral Home."

"I'll be there. Let me know if you need anything."

Without another word she was gone. Normally Abby would sit and talk for hours. I often felt I needed a navigation system to find a point in her conversations, but not today.

I went back to Felix's office and copied the "list" file to a new flash drive. I took the original and tucked it into a zippered compartment of my purse.

The growling in my stomach reminded me I hadn't eaten since breakfast, and that meal was long gone. I double checked that the house was locked up and walked into town to grab a bite.

Gil's Diner sat on the first floor of a brick building built in the mid-1800s. Although restored, the reclaimed brick and decorative trim still held its original charm.

I peeked through the big windows and saw Danny Lewis sitting at the counter. I walked through the door and wormed my way past the crowded tables and booths.

"Hey, Danny," I said, as I settled onto the stool next to him.

"Zoey!" Danny gave me a quick hug, the stubble from his grey beard rasping against my cheek. "I'm sorry 'bout Felix. When's the funeral?"

"Thanks. Friday at Christies," I said, as I read the specials posted on a whiteboard. "Danny, you and Felix had breakfast together almost every day, right?"

The waitress came by and refilled Danny's coffee cup. I ordered a grilled cheese and fries, all the time praying that this time my food would stay down.

Danny stirred his coffee, hitting his spoon against the cup. "Just 'bout. I just can't figure it." He took off his Tigers baseball cap and scratched his head.

"Figure what?"

He took a sip of coffee. "I overheard the cops sayin' it looked like an accidental death, but I don't know …"

I nodded as I took a bite of the sandwich the waitress delivered.

"What do you think, Danny? You found him." I swiveled the stool to face him.

He looked at me with bleary blue eyes. "Somethin' didn't sit right with me. You know what I mean?"

I nodded and looked around the restaurant. I could feel someone's eyes boring into me, but I didn't see anyone I recognized, or even anyone looking in my direction.

"Now, I'm not sayin' it wasn't his heart or anything, but, Zoey, his sleeping pills were by the bathroom sink. I've never seen them there before, and I've been to the house plenty. Somethin' don't seem right."

All the air left my body in a sharp gasp. I'd felt as if I'd been sucker punched in the gut. Of course, there wasn't a medicine cabinet in the bathroom, so Felix always kept his sleeping pills by his bed. I remembered always seeing them there.

"Like what?" I pushed my plate away. I'd lost my appetite.

"I don't know," he said and shook his head. "The last week or so Felix wasn't actin' like himself, you know? He was off. If I didn't know better, I would say he was scared. But with all those damn cases he was workin' on and people owing him money, who knows?"

I almost choked on my diet soda. "What people? Who owed him money?"

"A few people, I think. I saw him and someone arguin' 'bout it the other night on Felix's front porch when I took the dog for a walk."

"Who was it?" I said and leaned toward him.

"Don't know. It was dark, the porch light was off, and I was a ways from them. By the time I got up there, they were gone," he said and shrugged. "I have to go. The wife will be thinkin' I got lost. See ya Friday, Zoey." He tossed some money on the counter and left me sitting there with my mouth hanging open.

CHAPTER THREE

I wanted to process the day's events, so I took my time walking back to Felix's. I could swear I heard footfalls on the sidewalk behind me, but every time I turned around, no one was there. I arrived at the house to find Detective Andrews sitting in one of the Adirondack chairs on the front porch. Damn. This was the last thing I needed. I was tired, confused, and not in the mood for a confrontation.

When he saw me, he picked up his backpack and met me at the bottom of the porch stairs. "Miss Callaway."

"Please, call me Zoey. What do you want?" I said. He took my elbow and guided me up the stairs to the front door.

"I think we need to talk," he said. "Call me, Seth. Detective sounds so formal."

I sighed and took the keys out of my purse.

Karma greeted us at the door and followed us into the kitchen. He reached down to pet her, but she hissed and batted his hand away.

"Nice cat," he said, jerking his hand out of the way of her razor-sharp claws.

"Maybe she's as mad as I am that you took stuff out of the house."

"Yeah, about that," he said.

"Wine?" I took a bottle out of the fridge.

He nodded and took it out of my hand.

While he busied himself finding a corkscrew and two wine glasses, I took off my coat and turned on a few lights in the house.

He pulled out a chair for me at the kitchen table and we settled in with our wine.

"I'm sorry, Zoey." He leaned toward me in his chair. "I clearly didn't explain things well today. When we were here this morning, one of the officers saw items in your uncle's office that have to do with an open case. That's why we took them."

"Lacey Daniels?" I said, taking another sip of my wine.

"You knew your uncle was working on that?" he said, his dark eyes narrowed.

"Not until today. I was here last weekend and saw some girl's pictures on the whiteboard, but assumed it was a cold case. Now I wish I would have asked Uncle Felix about them." I set my wine glass down hard on the table. "If they're runaways, then what's the big deal? Kids run away all the time and show up a week or so later. And what's up with the FBI agent in the background of one of the news conferences?"

Seth's eyes flew open wide, his jaw dropped. "What the...?"

"You didn't know?" I said and sat back in my chair.

He got up to refill our wine glasses. "No, I didn't. How do you know?"

"I'm an information professional," I said.

"A what?"

"I'm a professional researcher. When I looked up one of the girl's names, there was a video of a news conference with her mother begging her to come home. In the background was an FBI agent I work for occasionally. So, what's really going on, Seth?"

"What other girls? What aren't you telling me, Zoey?" he said as he settled back down in his chair.

I sighed. "Felix sent me a package. I got it in the mail right before coming here this morning." I got up from the table and retrieved the flash drive that had a copy of the files on it and handed it to him.

"What's on it?" He tucked the flash drive into his backpack.

"A list of the girl's names." I avoided looking at him. Did he need the research file? Definitely. Did he need it right now? No.

"I'm assuming this is a copy?" he said and arched an eyebrow. I nodded.

"What else did Felix send you?"

"Nothing," I said, giving him a defiant glare.

"Okay, okay." He held his hands up, palms facing me. "Look, I'm just working on the case of a runaway from Hope Harbor. I don't have jurisdiction over the other cases."

"I see." I met his steady gaze with one of my own. "You know people owed Felix money, right? I spoke to someone today who said they heard a fight between Felix and someone else. Seth, I don't think my uncle's death was a suicide or accidental overdose. I think he was murdered."

He sat back in his chair. "That's quite a leap. Look, I'll check out what you told me, and we'll go from there."

I stretched and yawned. "I'd appreciate that."

"You've had a long day. I should go." He got up and put the wine glasses in the sink.

"Thanks for stopping by," I said as I walked him to the door.

"Again, I'm sorry for your loss. Make sure you lock the door," he said.

I closed the door behind him and turned the deadbolt into place. I glanced at the clock on the cable box and saw it was almost ten-thirty.

Before heading upstairs to the guest room, I took the flash drive out of my purse. When I got upstairs, I put it in the drawer of the nightstand.

As I got ready for bed, a profound sadness overtook me. I wished I could talk to Felix about everything that's happened. I got into bed and Karma snuggled in next to me, her soft purr bringing me comfort.

As hard as I tried, I couldn't sleep. I got out of bed around two a.m. and went downstairs. I stood at the bathroom door staring at the bathtub, trying to picture in my mind what happened to Felix.

I was finding it hard to concentrate because, being a rather neat person, I couldn't stand the dirt in the bathroom. It was making my skin crawl, so I got out a bucket, a gallon of bleach, and some rags I found in the laundry room and scrubbed the bathroom from floor to ceiling until everything was squeaky clean.

When I finished, I collapsed back into bed, exhausted.

I was awakened at seven a.m. by someone pounding on the front door and ringing the doorbell incessantly. Still half asleep, I stumbled down the stairs and opened the door – it was my mother.

She breezed past me and went through the living room to the kitchen.

"Why don't you have coffee ready?" she said.

"I was sleeping. What are you doing here? The funeral's not until tomorrow." I rubbed my eyes and went into the kitchen to make coffee. Karma followed me and sat on the floor looking up at her empty food dish on the kitchen counter. She gave out a loud meow.

"Where did that vermin come from?" Mom demanded, with her nose wrinkled in disgust.

I scooped Karma up in my arms and gave her a snuggle. "She's not vermin! This is Karma. Felix got her a couple weeks ago."

I set Karma on the kitchen counter and knowing how much it would piss off my mother, opened a can of food and dumped it in her bowl.

"On the kitchen counter? What are you thinking?" Mom yelled. "I trust you're taking it to the pound after the funeral."

No, I'm keeping her!"

"Not in your apartment you're not!"

Karma finished eating, so I set her on the floor, and she scampered off to play.

Mom grabbed her coffee and walked through the house. A few minutes later she rejoined me in the kitchen. "Didn't you even change the sheets on Felix's bed for me?"

"Mom," I said and sighed. "Sit down. I need to talk to you."

I told her about the events of yesterday and for once she really listened.

"Who would want to kill Felix?" She shook her head. "It makes no sense."

"I don't know why someone would kill him, but I'm going to find out," I said and sipped my coffee.

"No, Zoey, leave it to the police."

"The police think he died of natural causes, or maybe an accidental overdose." I held out my hands. "They aren't going to do anything unless I can find some more evidence."

"Just leave it be! No! Enough!" she said. "Now, let's get this place in livable shape."

And that was it. As far as she was concerned it was conversation over. That's how it worked in our family. We never discussed anything meaningful, we just swept it under the carpet and hoped it would go away.

Mom and I spent the rest of the morning sorting through Uncle Felix's belongings. We separated things into three piles: garbage, charity, and keep. Most of Felix's clothes went into the charity pile, and items like his war medals, commendations from the sheriff's department, and other miscellaneous items were in the keep pile.

We were cleaning out Felix's dresser when Karma walked into the room. She hunched down with her butt in the air and then, without warning, started racing around the bedroom like a maniac. She leapt from the floor to the bed, to the nightstand. When she hit the nightstand, the lamp, and magazines that'd been stacked neatly flew onto the floor. Then she jumped onto the dresser, sliding across the smooth surface. She managed to scatter the stacks of clothes onto the floor before running out of the room, leaving a path of destruction behind her.

"What the hell is wrong with that cat?" Mom said, a scowl on her face.

"I don't know. I've never seen her do that before." I cleaned up the mess and took six large bags of garbage outside.

When I had finished, I walked into the house and found my mom in Felix's office going through one of the file drawers.

"I already did this room, Mom," I said, leaning against the door jamb.

"Did you find his will?" she asked, glancing in my direction.

"I didn't even know he had one," I said and shrugged. "Why don't we see what's in the basement?"

We walked down the stairs to the basement, and saw it was in order, except for several boxes stacked in one corner. My mom and I looked at each other and sighed. "They can wait for another day," Mom said. For once, I couldn't argue with her and we went back upstairs and shut the basement door.

Mom settled on the couch to watch television and I went into the office to check my emails and get some work done.

In the early afternoon, I got a telephone call from Robert Simon, one of the four attorneys in town.

"Information by Zoey," I answered.

"Is this Zoey Callaway?" he said.

"Yes, it is. Did you need help with something?" I said.

"No, it has to do with your Uncle Felix. My condolences."

"Thank you," I said. "What about Felix?"

"Would it be possible for you to come by my office?" he said. I could hear the shuffling of papers in the background.

"Yes, of course. I can be there in a few minutes. Your office is above Gil's, right?" I said.

"Yes, see you soon," he said and hung up.

I sat for a moment staring at the phone. What the hell?

"I have to run an errand. I'll be back!" I said and escaped out the door and into my Jeep before she could reply.

I parked next to Gil's and walked to the alley behind the building. I opened the steel door to go up the staircase to his office.

I entered the reception area, and Mr. Simon was there to greet me.

"Zoey, good to see you. I just wish it was under better circumstances," he said shaking my hand.

"Yes, me too. Thanks," I said, shaking his hand. I noticed that instead of being dressed in his usual business suit, he was instead wearing a pair of jeans and a flannel shirt.

He led me into his office and motioned me into a high-backed leather chair across from his desk. I sat in silence as he opened a file and extracted a document.

"You know," he began. "Felix loved you more than life itself. I remember him going on and on about how proud he was of you when he came in to sign his estate documents."

Mr. Simon sat back in his chair, smoothing his grey hair with his hand.

"That's very kind of you to say," I said. "Oh, this is about his will? Should I call my mom? She's in town for the funeral," I said, reaching into my purse for my cell phone.

"No, that won't be necessary," he said, his eyes scanning the document before him. "It's pretty simple, really. Felix left you everything. The house, money, and all his possessions. Since everything was in a trust, and you're the only beneficiary, there won't be a need for the estate to go through probate." He paused and glanced up at me.

"What about my mom?" I said, leaning forward. I felt my stomach twist into a knot.

"He did mention her in his will," he said. "He told me he wasn't leaving her anything because he felt deserted by her. It seemed to upset him that she rarely called and hadn't visited him in years. However, he did soften a bit, and left her their grandfather's pocket watch."

"I understand. So, what do I need to do?" I said. I wanted to cry but couldn't decide if it was because Felix's death was so final now, or because I felt bad for my mom.

"Basically, you just need to sign these papers, and once you have the death certificate, go to Felix's bank and put your name on the accounts, or close them and open new ones, which would be my advice. I'll make several copies of the will and trust. The bank will want a copy." He set the documents in front of me and handed me a pen. "Felix also told me he had a life insurance policy. Is that correct?"

"Yes," I said, leaning forward. I tried to hide the fact that my hands were shaking when I signed the documents. "I found the policy among his things."

"Good, just call them, and they will tell you what you need to do. Of course, if you need any help, just let me know."

I slid the signed papers back across the desk to him. He excused himself and disappeared into another room and I heard the whirling of a copy machine.

While he was gone, I sat back in the chair and closed my eyes. I didn't want Felix's money, or his house. I didn't want any of it. I just wanted Felix back.

He returned a few minutes later and handed me a large envelope. "Everything you need is in here. Again, I'm sorry for your loss."

"Thank you," I said, taking the envelope from his hand. I left his office and drove into Briarwood, the county seat. I parked in a visitor's spot at the medical examiner's office and went inside where I was greeted by a young receptionist.

"Can I help you?" she said, her blonde ponytail swinging like a pendulum when she turned to look at me.

"Yes, I'd like a copy of my uncle's autopsy report," I said. "His name was Felix Callaway."

The receptionist punched in a few keys on her computer. "Are you next of kin?" she said, looking up at me with her brilliant blue eyes.

"Yes, I'm Zoey Callaway," I said, handing her a copy of the estate documents.

"Oh, Miss Callaway, the funeral home picked up your uncle an hour ago," she said as she looked through the documents I'd given her. "I'll get you a copy of the report." She left her seat and disappeared through a door to her left.

She returned a few minutes later with a file. "Here you go. I'm so sorry for your loss."

"Thank you," I said, taking the packet of papers from her.

I sat in my car and scanned through the report. Official cause of death was listed as an "accidental overdose." I read on: "extenuating circumstances – large amount of Eszopiclone in system." What was that?

I pulled out my cell phone and looked it up: it was the generic name for the brand of sleeping pill Felix took. The coroner also noted there was some water in his lungs. What the hell?

I flipped through the pages and found the pictures the coroner took at the scene. It showed Felix laying in the bathtub dead. There were pictures from various angles. I gasped and closed the report, taking a minute or two to collect myself. I took a deep breath and reopened the report, skimming through the pictures of Felix as fast as I could.

There was also a picture of the bathroom vanity with the bottle of sleeping pills on it. A close up of the bottle showed the prescription was in Felix's name.

I was interrupted by my cell phone.

"Hello?"

"Where the hell are you?" It was my mother. She was slurring her words. Just peachy.

"On the way home. I'll be there in a few minutes," I said and hung up.

I tucked the autopsy report into the envelope with the estate documents and headed home.

When I walked in the door, I found my mom siting on the couch swilling a glass of vodka, her drink of choice. There wasn't any vodka in the house, so where did she get it? She must have brought it with her. Of course.

"Where did you run off to so fast?" she said, her eyes trying to focus on me.

Before answering I put the envelope from the attorney on the desk in the office and returned to the living room. I sat down beside her.

"I was at Felix's attorney's office," I said, turning my face away from her. The smell of vodka on her breath was making me nauseous.

"Why didn't you tell me? I would have gone with you." she said, taking another swig out of her glass. "I'm sure he'll need to see me anyway."

"Actually Mom, no. He won't. Felix left everything to me," I said and braced myself for the explosion. But there wasn't one.

For the first time in my life, my mother was speechless. She sat with her mouth open, as if she wanted to speak, but no words came out. A lone tear trickled down her cheek. I almost felt sorry for her.

"I'm sorry, Mom," I said, putting my hand on her shoulder, which she swatted away as if it was a mosquito.

"What did I ever do that was so terrible?" she said and turned to face me. I could see fire burning in her eyes.

Here we go.

"What do you mean, Mom?"

"Felix." As she talked, her voice got louder.

"Could it be that you never visited and rarely called him?" Yes, we were going to go there.

"I'm busy. That's still no excuse for what he did!" She got to her feet and stood in front of me, a hand on her hip. She drained her glass of vodka and stomped into the kitchen to refill it. I followed her.

She stood with her hands on the kitchen counter, sobbing.

I put my arms around her and gave her a hug. For the first time in a long time, she hugged me back. I don't know how long we stood there, but when she let me go, she'd finished crying and was drawing in ragged breaths.

"Pour me another glass, Zoey. I need to go sit down." She turned away from me and went to sit on the couch in the living room.

I poured her a small glass of vodka and took it into her. "Felix did want you to have your grandfather's pocket watch," I told her.

"That's little consolation," she said.

I retreated to the kitchen to make something for dinner.

Mom joined me a few minutes later, and, after getting another glass of vodka, settled in at the table. "So, I suppose we're going to have to come back down here and get the house ready to sell."

"Mom, I'm going to move here," I said, and braced myself.

"Over my dead body!" Mom's face turned bright red. "You can't leave me like your father did."

"Mom, Dad died, he really didn't have a say in the matter. It's not the same thing."

"But what am I going to do?"

"What you always do, Mom, live your life. I won't be that far away," I said.

We ate the remainder of the meal in silence, and Mom, claiming she was exhausted, went to bed.

I felt restless, so I retrieved the flash drive and went into the office to try to get into the research file.

I went back through all the passwords to his online accounts in the file I'd found just to make sure I hadn't missed anything, but none of them worked.

Karma wandered into the room and climbed onto the desktop. I laughed as she chased the mouse pointer across the screen with her paw, and I remembered that last weekend Felix had shooed her away a few times for doing the same thing. Then it hit me: I was looking at the password.

I clicked on the file named "Research" and entered the password "Karma." I let out a squeal of delight when it worked.

There were three files in the folder; one labeled "Zoey," one labeled "Research," and one labeled "Pictures."

I clicked on the "Zoey" file and had to wait for the word processer to load before the document opened. It said:

Zoey,

I need your help. I should have talked to you about all of this when you were here last weekend, but I didn't want to get you involved unless it was absolutely necessary. If you're reading this, something has happened to me – I've either disappeared or am dead.

As you probably know by now, Lacey Daniels has dis-appeared. The police think she ran away, but I'm not so sure. Her father, Henry, has asked me to look into it, which I agreed to do.

Talk to Jax Cooper. He's a cop in Hope Harbo;, he's been helping me. You can trust him.

I'm sorry I can't tell you more, or make it easier for you, but I needed to take precautions, and it pains me

>to put you in harm's way, but you're the only one I can count on.
>
>Always remember that I love you with all my heart. You are the light of my life. I know with your skills you will figure all this out. Be careful my dear. If something happened to you, I'd never forgive myself.
>
>>Love,
>>Felix
>
>P.S. Please learn how to use a gun. You know where I keep my service pistol.

What the hell? I sat back in my chair and reread Felix's note several times to make sure I wasn't missing something.

I walked into the kitchen and poured a glass of wine. I needed to think about what Felix said.

Danny was right, Felix was scared, and judging by the tone of the letter, Felix knew something was going to happen to him, or at the very least, suspected as much. If this letter didn't convince the police, nothing would.

When I got settled back in the office, I opened the file labeled "Pictures." I saw images of teenagers hanging out in the park at night taken from some distance away. I clicked through the pictures examining each one. In a few of the photos I noticed the silhouette of someone standing in the shadows watching the kids, but I couldn't make out any details. Is this what Felix wanted me to see?

I looked at the time stamps on the pictures and then looked at them in the order they were taken. In the first few pictures the shadow man wasn't there, and then he seemed to appear out of nowhere. The next couple of photographs showed one of the kids approaching the man. Then, in the next series of photographs, they both disappeared from view. I couldn't make out who the kid was, but with a little work in Photoshop, I might be able to find out.

I managed to clean up one of the photos of the kids enough to make out that the kid who disappeared with the shadow man was a female, but try as I might, I couldn't make the picture of the man any clearer – he was in pitch blackness. I blew up the face of the girl and realized it was Lacey! The time stamp told me this was the night she disappeared!

I had to get these to the police! I pulled a fresh flash drive out of the desk drawer and copied the files before going to bed. As I tried to go to sleep, my mind was going so fast, I was having trouble forming a clear thought. Karma crawled up onto the bed with me and snuggled close, her purr lulling me to sleep.

CHAPTER FOUR

It took me forever to get ready for Felix's funeral in the morning. I knew I should wear my black dress, but it was a "little" black dress and I was pretty sure it wasn't appropriate to wear to a funeral, or a church.

I opted for a navy-blue skirt that wasn't too short, a white blouse, and the jacket that matched the skirt.

My mom wore the same black dress she'd worn to my father's funeral. Black wasn't really her color as it washed out her skin, but she'd plastered on some extra make-up in an attempt to look healthier – it didn't work.

We left for the funeral home earlier than we had to. We both wanted to have alone time with Felix before the rest of the mourners arrived. Barely a word had passed between us.

When we got to the funeral home, the funeral director, a portly man with pasty white skin, pulled me to the side and handed me a long envelope. "This is the death certificate. There's a few certified copies in case you need them."

"Thanks," I said. I ducked into an empty viewing room and pulled the document out of the envelope. It listed the same cause of death as the coroner's report. No surprise there. I thought back to the pictures of the scene the coroner included in his report. Something about them was bugging me, but I couldn't put my finger on it.

"Zoey!" I heard my mom yell.

"Coming!"

I ran out to my car before I joined my Mom in the viewing room and tucked the death certificates into the center console.

When I got to the door of the viewing room I stopped. Comfortable chairs and love seats in Victorian style were discreetly placed throughout the room in small groupings. Low tables with boxes of tissues and lamps on them sat in convenient places among the furniture. The room was bathed in a soft glow from the lamps and overhead lights.

Felix's casket sat straight ahead. The flowers I'd ordered were draped across the foot of the casket and the lid was open. My body started to tremble, and I felt like I was walking in wet cement as I made my way forward.

Felix looked so peaceful, I thought, as I stood before his baby blue casket. I wished I could hear his voice one more time, feel his arms wrap around me, and tell him all the things I wanted to. I thought I had more time to tell him how much he meant to me, how he was the only person who was ever really there for me. How much I loved him. I wiped away a stray tear as I turned away from the casket to greet the people coming in to pay their respects.

To me, it seemed as if most of the town turned out to mourn Felix. Mom and I kept busy greeting all the people and engaging in small talk, something I detest and fail miserably at.

When I was to the point where I couldn't thank anyone for their condolences anymore, I stepped outside for a small break. I saw Maddy Bartoni, Felix's housekeeper, hurrying up the sidewalk toward me. Over the years, we had become friends, and I was happy to see her slim frame approaching me. She looked beautiful in her plain black dress. Her short cropped blonde hair was neatly coifed as always, and her fingernails perfectly manicured.

"Zoey, I'm so glad I caught you," she said and gave me a quick embrace. "I know I probably shouldn't bring this up right now, but I was shocked when the newspaper said that Felix died of an accidental overdose."

"Yeah, me too. It's okay to talk about it. Maybe he was becoming more forgetful than I realized," I said and shrugged.

"No, he wasn't. I don't believe a word of it." Her green eyes focused on mine. "Felix set his watch to go off when it was time to take his medications, even his sleeping pill. The only way he could have overdosed is if he did it on purpose, and we both know he wouldn't do that."

I thought back on the time I'd spent with him and realized she was right. I'd forgotten about that. "Yes, I remember now. And you're right. Felix wouldn't take his own life."

"Are you going to sell the house?" she said.

"No, I'm moving here." I looked around and saw Seth pulling into a parking space.

"That's great!" she said with a bright smile. "We will have more time to spend together!"

"Yes, for sure. Can you excuse me?" I gave her a quick hug and hurried down the sidewalk to meet Seth.

"Hi, Zoey," he said.

"Hi. Listen, I found something. There's a letter to me from Felix, and pictures of teenagers in the park at night, and in one of the pictures you can see Lacey walk up to someone who was stand-ing in the shadows. It's the night she disappeared!"

"Zoey, get in here!" I heard my Mom call from the door of the funeral home.

"Coming!" I said.

Seth took my arm and walked with me up to the door. "I will need those."

"Stop by later today. I'll give them to you," I said.

The funeral service was filled with sentiment as many people shared their memories of Felix. I hadn't realized how much the town loved him. While my mom went with the mourners back to Felix's house for the wake, I followed the hearse to the cemetery.

I'd picked out a spot by one of the large oak trees that dot the cemetery landscape, and when we pulled through the wrought-iron gates at the entrance, I followed the hearse and parked.

With the help of the cemetery workers, Felix's casket was gently removed from the hearse and put on some type of mechanism.

I stood in stoic silence as the workers lowered Felix's casket into the ground. Out of the corner of my eye, I saw a stocky, well-built man standing next to a large oak tree a short distance away. He stayed in the shadows so I couldn't see his face, but I could feel his eyes boring into me with such intensity, that I fled to the safety of my SUV and left.

As I drove to Felix's house, I wondered who the man was. Damn it! Maybe it hadn't been my imagination; maybe someone did follow me home from Gil's the other night.

Felix's street was filled with cars and I was forced to park a street over and walk back to the house. One thing I loved about Hope Harbor was, when something happened, people rallied. Everyone had brought food, and I knew I would be eating left-overs for days. There were wall-to-wall people in the house, and

I worked my way through the crowd looking for Karma – she must have been freaking out.

I found her in my bedroom cowering under the bed. Once I had coaxed her out, I lay down on the bed with her and held her close. She took a soft paw and put it on my cheek. The sweet moment was shattered when I heard someone stomping up the stairs.

"What the hell are you doing up here with that damn cat? We have a house full of company! Really, Zoey!" My mother stood at the bedroom door with her hands on her hips.

After straightening my clothes, I joined my mother downstairs.

I went into the kitchen to help with the food, but was shooed out by Bea Perkins and some other women from the church. Aimlessly, I wandered through the house engaging in small talk with some of the mourners.

Many of Felix's buddies from the sheriff's department showed up, and I spent time listening to them reminisce about Felix.

The growling in my stomach reminded me I'd had nothing more than a piece of toast that morning. I walked over to the dining table and saw a platter of assorted lunch meat and cheese, so I made myself a sandwich and sat down on the end of the couch so I could put my plate on the end table.

Pam Davidson, the president of the Hope Harbor Historical Society came and sat down next to me.

"I'm going to miss Felix," she said. "He was always such a huge supporter of the Historical Society. Came to all the events. He was a lot of fun."

"Thank you. Felix would talk about the good time he had at one event or another," I said, taking a bite of my sandwich.

"He was very proud of you," she said. "So much so that he recommended you for a project, and at the last board meeting we decided to offer you the job – if you want it of course."

"What is it?" The distraction would do me good.

"Now's not the time to talk about it, dear," Pam said and patted my hand. "I'll call you later in the week and we'll set up a time to meet."

"Sounds good. Thanks. Please excuse me, I have to help my Mom in the kitchen," I said rising from my seat. Pam could talk for days and I'd spotted Seth and another man come through the front door.

I pulled them both aside and took them into Felix's office.

"Zoey, this is Jax, an officer on the force," Seth said.

The man Felix told me to find! Perfect!

"Hi," I said and shook his hand. "Felix spoke of you often. I think he was fond of you."

"That's nice of you to say, thank you." He shook my hand and his dark eyes met mine.

"You two have to see this," I said putting the flash drive in my computer. I pulled up the picture I'd cleaned up with Lacey and the mystery man. "Look at the time stamp, it has to be the night Lacey disappeared."

Seth and Jax studied the photograph.

"She knew him," Jax whispered.

Seth nodded. "This changes everything."

"I'm going to need that flash drive," Seth said.

"All yours," I said and pulled the drive out of the slot in the computer and handed it to him. "Now do you think my uncle died from an accidental overdose? There's more than enough evidence on there to reopen Felix's case." I gave him a hard stare.

"What else is on here?" Seth said.

"A letter from Felix to me. He knew something was going to happen to him," I said.

Seth sighed. "I'll review it, but I can't promise anything."

Before I could respond, Seth's cell phone rang, and he walked out of the room as he answered.

"I'm sorry, Zoey. Your uncle was a good guy. I wish there was something I could do," Jax said.

"There is," I said, remembering what Felix said in his letter.

"You can teach me how to shoot a gun. I'm terrified of them."

His dark eyes searched my face to see if I was serious. He ran his hand through his curly black hair and shuffled his feet.

"You don't have to. It's okay," I said.

"No, no. I'll help you," he said. "There's a gun shop down on Harper. They have a range in the back. Give me your number, I'll set something up and call you."

"Thanks," I said and gave him an impulsive hug.

"We have to go," Seth said, as he came back into the room.

We walked out of the office and joined the other guests. I jotted down my number for Jax and handed it to him as they were leaving.

I spent the rest of the day playing hostess with my mom. By six o'clock everyone was gone, and I collapsed on the couch. Maddy stayed to help clean the kitchen and straighten up the house.

My mom emerged from the bedroom a few minutes later with her suitcase in tow.

"Mom, where are you going?" I got up off the couch and walked over to her.

"I'm leaving. I told you I have plans for tomorrow and I have to get ready," she said. She looked tired and a lot older than her fifty years.

"But, Mom, I thought you'd stay, at least until morning." The truth was I didn't want her to leave. I felt lost and overwhelmed. My mother, even though we didn't see eye to eye on anything, brought me some comfort and was the only family I had left.

"No." Her eyes hardened. "You've made your intentions very clear, Zoey. I'll expect you to have your things out of the apartment by the end of the month so I can get it ready to rent."

Before I could respond, she walked out the door, slamming it hard behind her. I stood looking after her with tears streaming down my face. I felt like an abandoned puppy.

Maddy and I exchanged looks from across the room. She crossed the distance between us in four long strides and enveloped me in a hug. "I'm so sorry, Zoey. Would you like me to stay?"

"No, I'll be fine," I said.

"I'll get us some wine. Go sit down on the couch," she said and disappeared into the kitchen. She emerged a few minutes later and joined me.

I filled her in on everything that happened. She listened, never taking her eyes off me. When I finished, she sat back in her seat processing the information.

"I believe you. What can I do to help?" she said.

"I'm not sure yet," I said, staring into my wine glass.

She nodded. "Do you think Felix's death and Lacey's disappearance are related?"

Karma had found the courage to come downstairs and walked into the living room mewing.

"I'm not sure," I said getting up from the couch. I walked into the kitchen with Karma hot on my heels. I filled her food and water bowls. "It's possible."

I let that theory play itself out in my head. Right now, it was the only thing that made sense.

"You've had a rough few days. Why don't you let it be for a while? Go back to your mom's, get your stuff and get settled. Maybe something will turn up."

"That's not a bad idea," I said and stretched.

She took my wine glass and disappeared into the kitchen. "I'll stay here with Karma while you're gone and give the house a good cleaning."

"Thanks. I'll want to keep you on as my housekeeper if you're interested," I said as we walked to the front door.

"Of course." We hugged, and I locked the door behind her.

As I shut the blinds before going upstairs, I saw someone standing on the sidewalk across the street staring at the house. I couldn't make out any features, but he had the same silhouette as the man in the cemetery.

A cold shiver ran down my spine. I snapped the blinds shut and turned off the lights. I eased a blind slat up with my finger and peered outside. The man was gone.

I double checked the windows and doors to make sure they were locked before heading up to bed.

CHAPTER FIVE

In the morning, I packed up and headed back to my apartment. I spent the next few days in a whirlwind of packing and arranging for the movers to take my stuff to Felix's house. I was excited, but the circumstances behind Felix's death and Lacey's disappearance nagged at the back of my mind.

I tried to stay out of the way as the movers loaded my things into the truck. I wasn't taking any furniture, but my collection of first edition books and my clothes had grown considerably in the last couple of years and I didn't want to lug everything by myself.

Just as the movers were carrying out the last of the boxes, my cell phone pinged. I pulled it out of my pocket and saw a text from a number I didn't recognize. It said: "Bad things happen to little girls who don't mind their own business."

I let out a gasp. Normally something like this would scare the crap out of me, but today it only pissed me off. Who sent this? Maybe it had to do with my work on Project Shadow for the FBI. After all, I did have to enter the nefarious world of the dark web to gather some of the information I needed for that assignment.

I made a mental note to double check the firewalls on my computer when I got home and tucked my phone in my pocket.

Before leaving for Hope Harbor I wrote a note to my Mom telling her I loved her and to come visit anytime. We both knew it would never happen, but I had to put forth the effort. I put the keys and note in an envelope and dropped it through the mail slot in her front door. I didn't see the point to a prolonged and drama-filled goodbye.

When I arrived home, Maddy greeted me at the door with Karma in her arms. While I was away, she'd arranged to have the donations picked up, had deep cleaned the whole house, and painted my office a pretty shade of robin's egg blue.

We ordered pizza and spent the rest of the day unpacking. She left around nine, and I was exhausted. I picked up Karma and took her up to bed. I fell asleep to her loud purr reverberating through my chest.

The next morning, I felt like death warmed over. My head ached, and I was stiff and sore. I forced myself to go for a run, but only made it three miles instead of my usual five.

After getting cleaned up, I walked into Felix's bedroom. It felt as if time had stood still. His heavy black comforter covered the bed, and his bathrobe and pajamas were hanging on the hook behind his bedroom door.

I walked over to the nightstand next to his bed. When I opened the drawer, there it lay – Felix's pistol. Just looking at it made my hands sweat, and a cold chill ran down my spine.

In my mind, I could still hear the gunshot that killed my father echo through the basement of my mother's house. I remembered my mother's scream, the blood, and my dad's head blown apart.

I pushed away the memories and held out a shaking hand to grab the gun. The holster was soft and worn with the outline of the gun ingrained into the dark brown leather. I took a deep breath and opened the holster to withdraw the weapon. The gun felt cold in my trembling hand, and I realized I was holding my breath.

"It's not going to bite, Zoe," I said aloud. "Get a grip."

I got my hand to stop shaking, which I figured was enough for today. I put the gun back into the holster and closed the drawer to the nightstand.

"I'm such a wimp," I said to Karma as she followed me out of the bedroom.

I got my cell phone out of my purse and called Jax. He agreed to meet me at the gun shop and gave me directions.

It took everything I had to take the gun out of the drawer and tuck it into my purse before heading out to meet Jax. "This is going to be a disaster," I whispered to myself as I found a place to park at the gun shop.

Jax was waiting for me when I walked through the door.

"Hey, you ready?" he said and smiled.

I managed a weak nod, and he led me to unfamiliar territory – the large back room of a gun shop staring at a paper target with the black silhouette of a man on it.

"Give me the gun, I need to make sure it's in good working order before you shoot it," Jax said.

I reached into my purse and handed him Felix's revolver.

"You know," Jax said, as he inspected Felix's weapon. "I think Seth was a little put out that you didn't ask him to teach you to shoot."

"Why?" I said. "What did he say?"

"It's not what he said." Jax slid a full clip of bullets into the gun until it locked into place. "It's what he didn't say."

"I'll apologize to him later," I said and sighed.

"Don't apologize. You didn't do anything wrong." Jax handed me the gun. "Okay, I think we're all set."

He moved behind me, his arms over mine to help me steady my hands.

"The trick," he said, "is to exhale just as you pull the trigger. Squeeze it gently and try to keep yourself still. Bend your elbows a little to absorb any kickback and relax."

I nodded and set my feet, bent my elbows, and tried to settle myself down. Jax stepped to the side.

"Very good. Now, pull the trigger."

I squeezed the trigger and screamed as the sound of the shot echoed through the room. The gun hit the counter in front of me and bounced to the floor. Jax grabbed me and pulled me out of the line of fire in case the gun went off.

"Not bad for your first time," he said, a ghost of a smile playing around his mouth.

I crinkled my nose at him.

He picked up my gun and put on the safety before handing it back to me. "Now, try again."

He turned out to be a patient teacher – well, let's just say he had more patience than I would have had and before long I was getting more comfortable handling the weapon and even managed to hit the target a couple of times.

When we finished shooting, he taught me how to disassemble the gun, clean it, and reload the clip.

"I can't thank you enough," I said as we walked out of the gun shop to our cars.

"Any time," he said and smiled. "We'll meet up again in a couple of days to give you some more practice."

"That would be great. Thanks." I pulled my cell phone out of my purse. "What do you make of this?" I showed him the mysterious text and saw a grim expression cross his handsome face as he read it.

"I don't like this, Zoey. You've rattled someone's cage. Exactly whose business have you been sticking your nose into?" he said.

"I can't say. Client confidentiality, but I'll be more careful," I said.

"I'm going to keep a close eye on your place while I'm on duty. Call me if you need me and I'll be right there," he said as he unlocked the door to his pickup truck.

"I really appreciate it. Thanks, Jax."

I had a few errands to run before heading home, so I locked Felix's gun in the center console before pulling out of the parking lot of the gun shop.

On the way to the grocery store Pam Davidson called and asked if I could meet her at the historical society this evening. I agreed and was rather excited about this new project here in town.

I got to the store and noticed there was a rather large cat climbing tree on sale, so I threw caution to the wind and bought that too. Maybe it would keep Karma from climbing the drapes in the living room.

By the time I got home, put away the groceries, and lugged Karma's new kitty jungle gym into the house it was late afternoon. I checked my email, transferred client payments into my checking account, and took a nap before heading into town to meet Pam.

The Hope Harbor Historical Museum is housed in an old hotel built in 1881. After the innkeeper died, his widow ran it for a few years before selling it to her brother, who turned it into a boarding house. It changed hands a few times throughout the years before being sold to the historical society and turned into a museum.

The two-story building was constructed of reclaimed brick, most of which was made right here in Hope Harbor. Two bay windows jutted out from the face of the building on either side of the doors. One of the doors led to the museum, while the other one led to a storefront that housed Dixon's Bookstore, one of my favorite places.

I saw lights on in the museum, so I climbed the three worn cement steps and opened the heavy wooden front door. When I walked into the museum, the stairway to the second floor was in front of me along with a hallway that led toward the back of the building. To my right was a gift shop. I entered the gift shop and saw large pictures of Hope Harbor's past on the walls, and a couple of display cases filled with books, T-shirts, and other items the museum sold to raise money.

The gift shop gave way to a generous sized dining room with a long dining table and various displays.

When I walked in, Pam Davis was sitting at the table in the dining room with a man I didn't recognize.

"Right on time," she said. "This is Jason Brock. Jason, meet Zoey."

Jason stood up from his chair to shake my hand. He was built like a tank, a bit on the short side and extremely muscular. "Nice to meet you."

"You too," I said, as I put my purse on the table and sat down in a high-backed wooden chair. I pulled a small notebook and pen out of my purse and rested my hands on the table.

"Jason just moved here recently, and already we don't know what we'd do without him. In fact, he was just voted onto the board," Pam said, giving him a big grin. "Zoey just moved here too, although she's been here many times visiting her uncle."

"I see," Jason said, his blue eyes meeting mine.

"Welcome to the neighborhood," I said, holding his gaze.

"So, tell me about this cemetery," I said.

"Well," Jason said, sliding a file folder toward me. "We honestly don't know much. From what the developer told us, it's quite small. Maybe fifteen to twenty graves is all."

"Okay," I said, writing a few notes.

Pam leaned towards me. "We're kind of hoping it's the witch cemetery."

"The witch cemetery?" I said. I'd never heard of such a thing.

"Jason's taken a special interest in this project. He's particularly interested in old cemeteries, so this project is kind of his baby," Pam said, patting Jason's shoulder.

"Yes," Jason said. "According to my research, in the late 1700s and into the early 1800s, many people were still fearful of witches. From what I understand, several women in the area were accused of witchcraft. Now, we can't find any records of witch trials or anything like that, but it's been rumored that, when these women died, they weren't allowed to be buried at Oakmont Cemetery in town, so the families buried them in a secret location."

"Interesting," I said. "Sad, too."

"It is." Pam nodded her head. "These papers contain all the information we have and the GPS coordinates for the cemetery. We're so excited to see what you find!"

"Me too! So, what exactly do you want me to do?" I reached into my messenger bag and pulled out a file that held two copies of my contract.

"We want you to identify the people buried there and do some research on each person to find out what you can about them. We don't need the entire genealogy, but we'd like to at least know something about them," Pam said.

"I can do that," I said, transcribing the scope of work onto the contracts before handing them to Pam.

She took the contract and read it over before signing both copies and giving one copy back to me.

"Thanks," I said and gathered the papers together. I tucked everything in my purse and got up to leave.

"Now, you let me know if you need anything, or just want to talk," she said, getting to her feet.

"I'll walk with you part way. I'm meeting a friend at the Blue Bass on the corner," Jason said. He got up and grabbed his coat off the back of his chair.

He followed me to the front door and opened it for me.

As we walked through town, we talked about the cemetery and who may be buried there.

"Let me know if you need anything," he said. "I'd really like to help. I'm fascinated by the place."

"I will. Thanks."

We'd reached the Blue Bass restaurant, and after we said good bye, Jason disappeared inside. As I walked the short distance home, I thought about what Pam had said about the cemetery. I couldn't wait to get started on this project!

When I was almost to the front door, I fished for my keys in my purse. Why didn't the motion sensor turn on the porch light? I had just changed the bulb a week or so ago. I waved my hand in front of the sensor, but no luck. I reached my hand into the light fixture and realized the bulb had been removed. The hair on the back of my neck rose, and I stood perfectly still listening for any movement, but was met only by the sound of crickets.

I looked up and down the street, but nothing seemed out of place. In my rush to open the door, I fumbled with my keys, until I finally got the right one into the lock. I went to walk into the house and the toe of my shoe touched something and pushed it aside. I turned on a light in the foyer to see what it was. A small white box tied with a piece of string sat on the welcome mat. I looked again at the empty light socket on the porch. What the hell?

I picked up the package, walked into the kitchen, and sat my things down on the dining table. I'd remembered seeing spare bulbs in the front closet, so I replaced the bulb on the porch, checked its operation, and shut and locked the door.

By the time I got back to the kitchen, Karma was on the table pawing at the box and meowing incessantly. I untied the string and removed the lid. Whatever was inside the excessive tissue paper was soft. Gingerly I pulled back a piece of the tissue paper and saw a tiny black sightless eye staring at me. An open beak gaped. The sparrow was dead. Its severed head was now resting on the bird's belly and was held in place by the bird's wings which had been safety pinned together.

CHAPTER SIX

I let out a scream that sent Karma scrambling off the table, to the top level of her scratching post. I slammed the lid back on the box, and put my hands on the table, gasping for breath.

Just then I heard my phone ping. The text said: Did you like my little present? Holy crap, had he seen me come home? I hadn't seen anyone, but that didn't mean anything. It was pitch black outside and there were tons of trees and bushes someone could hide behind. I ran through the house double-checking all the windows and doors and closing all the blinds.

I wanted to text back but thought better of it. The last thing I wanted to do was encourage this guy, but this had to stop. The bird was obviously a threat, but the question was who sent it and why? I put the box with the dead bird in it inside a plastic storage bag and placed it in the freezer.

I went into Felix's bedroom and opened the nightstand drawer to get his gun. As I picked it up, the same old feelings of fear ran through me, and I put it away.

I poured a glass of wine and headed into my office – Karma started racing around the house doing her cat zooming trick again, and I sighed as I heard things falling off of shelves.

A short search on the internet told me the dead bird either meant death, rebirth, or was a sign of organized crime. Hmmm... right now I was involved in Felix's death and organized crime based upon my research for Project Shadow. They couldn't afford a horse's head? I chuckled to myself.

I double checked my firewalls to make sure they hadn't been breached and that I was still invisible on the internet before settling in to go through my email.

I realized I'd been so preoccupied with Felix's death that my clients were being ignored. It was the middle of the night before I finished the last job, invoiced the clients, and shut off my computer. I picked up the things Karma had knocked off the mantle of the fireplace and the side table in the living room before turning off the lights.

Wearily, I climbed the stairs to my bedroom and was asleep before my head hit the pillow.

In the morning after a quick breakfast, I double-checked to make sure I had my digital camera, tape recorder and notepad. Redundancy was everything in my line of work and losing any information, once gathered, was unthinkable. Hence, the span from old to current technology.

I opened the front door to leave and found Seth standing right in front of me with a banker's box in his hands.

"What are you doing here?" I said, backing into the house to let him enter.

"I brought back your uncle's laptop and some of the files we took."

"Great, can you just set them on the kitchen table?"

Seth walked through the living room and deposited the box on the table. "Where are you off to?"

"An old cemetery," I said. "The historical society hired me to investigate it."

"Have fun, but be careful," he said, walking back toward the front door. "Any word from your stalker?"

"No, maybe he got bored," I said as I grabbed my keys out of my purse.

"I doubt that. Want me to come with?"

"Don't be silly, I'm perfectly capable of taking care of myself." I walked to my vehicle and tossed my messenger bag on the front seat.

"You sure about that?" he said before walking back to his pickup truck.

"Positive," I called after him.

I followed the GPS directions out of town, and a short time later pulled my Jeep into a barely visible two-track. I drove into the woods as far as I could. When the road ended, I gathered my things and locked up the truck. I'd have to walk the rest of the way.

When I entered the thick forest, it seemed to come alive. I could hear the cawing of ravens, and the sound of robins and red-winged black birds. Squirrels rustled through the carpet of fall leaves that lay on the forest floor, and they hurried out of my way as I walked. The musky air smelled like damp ground, fallen leaves, and white pine. I breathed deeply, enjoying the aroma.

A short time later, I saw a clearing ahead of me dotted with large oak trees. As I left the denseness of the forest, the cemetery came into view.

I stepped into the eerie quiet of the magnificent century old oak trees whose canopies loomed over the old granite and limestone grave markers. The sounds of the forest had fallen quiet, and the silence was almost deafening. I wondered where all the animals had gone. A wispy mist snaked its way around the tombstones causing the cemetery to look like something out of a horror movie.

"Get a grip, Zoe," I said and set my stuff down. I pulled out my camera, tape recorder, notebook and pen and got to work.

Some of the tombstones were so weather worn, that, if I couldn't clean up the images on my computer, I'd have to return and do rubbings of some of the stones and then try to decipher the information.

I began to move methodically through the graveyard snapping pictures and recording both on my tape recorder and notepad.

As I worked, the feeling I was being watched gave me goosebumps, and I stopped several times to look around and listen for any movement.

The last row of grave markers sat away from the rest, and, as I worked my way toward them, a ray of sunshine glinted off something lying against one of the small stones with a carved lamb on top of it, indicating it was the grave of a baby or young child.

I walked over to the grave marker and saw that the shiny object was a chain and locket. I set down my messenger bag and reached out a gloved hand to examine it. I turned it over and saw the word, "Lacey" engraved on the front.

A knot formed in the pit of my stomach. I sat cross legged on the ground and took a deep breath. How the hell did Lacey's locket get out here? Unless…

I used my cell phone to snap some pictures of the locket and then called Seth.

He answered on the third ring. "Hey, Zoey. What's up?"

"Seth," I said in a hushed tone. "I'm at the cemetery and I found Lacey's locket by one of the tombstones. You need to get out here." Why was I whispering?

"You what? Where are you exactly?" he said. I could hear the tenseness in his voice.

"I'll text you the GPS coordinates. It's in the forest off Ridge Road."

"I'm on the way." The line went dead.

I texted Seth the directions and a picture of the locket.

I could hear sirens in the distance, and, knowing I needed to stay away from the scene, I walked around the perimeter of the cemetery. As I did, I noticed a small trail not far from the locket leading deeper into the woods. Just as I was about to follow it, I heard people crashing between the branches. I looked up to see Seth, Jax, and crime techs entering the cemetery.

"Where is it?" Seth said, his eyes looking me over.

"Over there," I said and pointed.

Seth nodded and walked away. I saw him stoop down and look at the locket before motioning to the crime techs.

"Someone went into the woods this way," I said, walking over to the trail with Seth in tow. "Come on." I started to head up the path.

Seth grabbed my arm. "Where do you think you're going?"

"I'm going to follow it." I yanked my arm out of his grasp.

"I don't think so," he said. "There may be evidence on the trail that you could compromise. Let us take care of it. Why don't you go home; Jax will walk you back to your car."

"That won't be necessary," I said, flashing Jax a smile. "I know the way."

I put my stuff away, picked up my messenger bag and trudged back through the woods. I was disappointed that I hadn't been able to follow the trail, but he was right – if there was evidence the less people who went trampling through the woods the better. What nagged at my mind was why Lacey would go that deep into the woods? Was she hiding out somewhere?

CHAPTER SEVEN

I got home and unpacked my messenger bag. After making some coffee and changing into yoga pants and a sweatshirt, I sat down at my desk to organize all the data I'd collected from the cemetery.

I knew I'd started at the front of the cemetery and the graves were in rather neat rows. I opened my spreadsheet program, grabbed my notebook, and started to enter the names on the graves, labeling them by row into my spreadsheet. When I came to the stones I couldn't read, I put in a place marker.

After getting another cup of coffee, I took the SD card out of my digital camera and slipped it into the computer to review the pictures. I was able to fill in a few more names, but there were still a few stones I'd have to take rubbings from to glean any information.

I pulled out the file Pam and Jason had given me and compared the names on my spreadsheet to the few names they'd discovered. They were a match! This was the witch's cemetery, alright, but I still had questions. Were the other people in the cemetery also considered to be witches or warlocks? Judging by the names on the graves, a lot of the people were part of the same family. More research would be needed. I fired off a quick email to Pam telling her the good news and asking if she'd pass the information along to Jason.

Just as I hit send my cell phone rang. It was Jax.

"Hey, Jax," I said as I got up to make more coffee. Karma followed me into the kitchen and climbed onto the counter. She sat down and stared at me.

"Hi, Zoey. Listen, I'm not going to be able to make shooting practice today. We found Lacey Daniels' body out by the ceme-tery you were at earlier," he said, his voice almost a whisper. "If you hadn't found that necklace, we may never have found her."

I drew in a ragged breath. "Oh my God, that's terrible."

"Yeah, it's pretty bad. Seth's on his way over to the Daniels' house right now." I could hear the muted sounds of people talking in the background, and the wind whistling through the trees. "Thanks for letting me know."

I heard someone call his name.

"I'll talk to you later. I have to go," he said and hung up.

I stood at the kitchen counter staring into space. With Felix's death still so fresh in my mind and now Lacey's murder, it was too much. I buried my face in my hands and wept.

Stop it, Zoe! I told myself. Crying solves nothing, it's time to dig in and get some answers. I washed my face and went back to my office.

I ordered a luncheon tray to be sent to the Daniels' house from Swenson's Deli in town and then settled in to see if I could find Lacey's cell phone.

After opening one of the programs I use I punched in Lacey's number. Seconds later a map appeared on the screen with a blip showing that her phone was about twenty miles away from the cemetery. What the hell? I printed out the map and put the GPS coordinates into my phone.

On the way out of town, I went by Felix's bank and closed his accounts. I opened new ones and had the money transferred into them. Then I mailed the information the life insurance company needed to process the claim.

I followed the GPS to where it indicated Lacey's phone should be. I ended up two towns over, standing on a pier that overlooked the St. Clair River. The GPS said the last place Lacey's phone pinged off a tower was two hundred feet ahead of me, which meant her phone was at the bottom of the waterway. *Isn't that convenient?* I thought.

By the time I got home the sun was just starting to set so I showered and locked up the house before setting out on the two-block walk to the Daniels' house. The driveway and street were filled with cars. I walked up to the front porch and rang the doorbell. Henry Daniels answered.

"Zoey," he said, giving me a hug. "Thank you for the tray. Please, come in."

He took my coat and hung it in the coat closet. "Come with me," he said as he took my elbow and led me into his den, shutting the door behind us.

He motioned me into a chair and sat down across from me at his desk. His shoulders slumped, and his eyes looked vacant, empty, as if his soul had been sucked out of his body.

"Henry, I'm so sorry. What can I do to help?" I said.

"You can find out who killed Lacey," he said and wiped his face with his hand.

"That's up to the police. You know that." I leaned forward in my chair.

"The detective that was here told the wife and I that you were the one that found her necklace," he said.

Damn you, Seth. You are so going to hear about this.

"Yes, but it was just a coincidence. I was just in the right place at the right time, so to speak," I said, noticing his lips were quivering.

I got up from my chair and walked around his desk. I wrapped my arms around his shoulders and gave him a hug. He rested his head against my chest and sobbed. I held him tight until he collected himself.

"Please, Zoey. Your uncle was looking into Lacey's case before he died. People will talk to you. You notice things others don't. Just keep your eyes and ears open. That's all I'm asking. I'll pay you whatever you want," he pleaded.

"I don't want your money, Henry. I will do what I can," I said. "Tell me about the day Lacey disappeared."

Henry sat back in his chair and closed his eyes. "It was a normal day. Lacey and I had breakfast. Jill wasn't up yet. She asked me for a ride to school, so I dropped her off. When she got out of the car she said, 'love you, Dad.' It was the last time I saw her, but it was odd."

"In what way?"

"I've dropped her off at school hundreds of times, but this was the first time she told me she loved me before she got out of the car."

"So, you think she was planning something? Like meeting someone, or running away?"

"I don't know," Henry said and shrugged. "But something changed a couple of weeks ago. I talked to some of her friends right after she disappeared, and they even said that Lacey had been acting differently. They said she told them she had a new boyfriend who didn't go to their school. She'd met him online, and he was older. I didn't know anything about it. How could I not know, Zoey?" He buried his face in his hands.

"She was a teenager. But the online boyfriend is concerning," I admitted. "Is her computer here?"

"The police took it," he said. "I don't know what they found."

"That doesn't surprise me. Detective Andrews is not real forthcoming with information. I'll see what I can do," I said and sighed.

We walked into the living room and joined the other mourners. I noticed Seth and Jax standing off to one side sipping sodas, their eyes scanning the crowd.

I chased Henry's wife, Jill, out of the kitchen and took over the job of making sure the guests were fed, picked up empty plates and glasses, and loaded the dishwasher.

I noticed Jill walk past the guests as if she were in a trance and sit down in a chair in the corner of the living room. My heart went out to her, and I wanted to just scoop her up in my arms and hold her, but nothing would take away the pain she was feeling. As sad as I was about Felix, I couldn't even fathom the depth of her sorrow and grief over losing her daughter.

It was after 10 p.m. before everything was cleaned up and the last of the guests left. Jill had been given a sedative by her doctor, and she was in her bedroom resting – probably the best thing for her.

"Do you want me to drive you home?" Henry asked as I wiped the kitchen counters one more time.

"No, I can walk, but thanks." I gathered my coat and bag and gave him a hug before heading out into the darkness.

As I walked toward home, I was so far down the rabbit hole thinking about Lacey's death, it took a heavy footfall on the sidewalk behind me to drag me back to reality.

I turned around and saw Jason a few steps behind me. "Are you following me?"

"No," he said. "Just heading home."

He caught up to me in three long strides. "Pam called and said you confirmed the graveyard is the witch cemetery."

"Yes, but there's also a few members of the same family buried out there, as well," I said, thrusting my hands into my coat pockets.

"Interesting. Which family?"

"The Rockman's. Do you know about them?"

"I don't know much about them, but I'll look into it and ask Pam," he said.

"Great. Let me know."

We stopped on the sidewalk to exchange cell phone numbers and then continued our walk.

"This is me," I said as we got to my house. "Thanks for walking with me."

"You're welcome. Have a good night."

I let myself into the house and just as I was about to shut the door, I saw Jason disappear into the house across the street. What the hell? I didn't know he lived next to Danny Lewis.

Not being particularly tired, I poured a glass of wine and headed into my office to check my email. A couple of work orders from clients had come in. Good, maybe it would take my mind off things for a bit. There was also an email from Dixon's Bookstore, telling me the book I wanted was in and I could pick it up anytime.

I'd just started to get to work when my cell phone pinged. It was a text from my stalker. "What kind of wine are you drinking?"

What the hell? I looked up and realized I hadn't shut the blinds in the office. I turned off my desk light and computer monitor and looked out the window. In the light of the moon I could just make out the silhouette of someone standing by a tree. I snapped the blinds shut and sat back in my chair breathless. Damn pervert.

I turned on my desk lamp and monitor and started to work. One hour and two glasses of wine later, I sat back in my chair and stretched. I turned off my computer and rinsed out my wine glass. I was plugging my cell phone into the charger on my nightstand when another text pinged on my phone. "Are you sure you locked the door?"

Chills ran up and down my spine. Did I? I tiptoed to the top of the stairs and not wanting to turn on a light, clutched the railing as I made my way to the front door – one dark step at a time. I checked the door; both locks were engaged. "Whew," I said and with my back against the door, slid down to the floor. A few minutes later I picked myself up and, after grabbing the fireplace poker, made my way up to bed.

CHAPTER EIGHT

The next morning, I decided to stop by Dixon's Bookstore and get the book I'd asked for. Felix and I had been going to Dixon's since I was a little girl. Frank Dixon, who owned the store, was a retired librarian and somewhat of a gossip.

Frank looked up when the bell on the shop door rang.

We exchanged greetings as I headed for the mystery section of the shop.

I perused the shelves, tilting my head so I could read the titles. My hair kept falling into my eyes, and I paused to pull it back in a ponytail.

Finally, seeing what I was looking for, I stood on tiptoes and stretched my arm as far as it would go, but I still couldn't reach the book. I heard Frank chuckle as he walked over and easily grabbed the book off the second shelf from the top and handed it to me.

"Thanks," I said as I opened the cover to look at the copyright page.

"Moving from Sherlock to Nero Wolfe?"

"I thought I'd give him a try," I said as I followed him up to the cash register. "I need to pick up the book you found for me too."

"Got it right here," he said and reached under the counter.

He laid it on the counter, and I noticed he'd already wrapped the dust jacket in an archival quality clear protector for me.

I pulled a pair of white cloth gloves out of the bowl next to the register and put them on before picking up the book to examine it. The first edition, first printing of *The Great Gatsby*, by F. Scott Fitzgerald had been on my wish list forever. It'd taken me months to save up enough money to buy it, and as I examined the book, I realized it'd been worth every penny.

"I was stunned to hear about Lacey Daniels," Frank said and shook his head. "Nasty business, that."

"Yes, it is," I said, setting the book back on the counter and removing the gloves.

"I went over there last night, but you were so busy in the kitchen I didn't get a chance to talk to you," he said as he wrapped my book in wispy layers of tissue paper.

"I wanted to do something to help," I said.

Frank nodded. "Looks like you've picked up an admirer."

Butterflies fluttered in my stomach as I thought about the nasty texts. "What do you mean?"

"Jason Brock. He couldn't take his eyes off you," he said and chuckled. "You could do worse you know. He seems like a decent fella. Comes in here once a week or so to pick up a mystery or true crime book."

"Really?" The thought of Jason watching me gave me the creeps.

"Course, he's not a serious collector like you, but it's a start," he said as he stroked his white beard.

"Are you playing matchmaker now?" I said and grinned as I handed him my debit card.

"No," he said, his cheeks and ears turning bright red. "Just a thought."

"Well, I appreciate the effort, Frank." I picked up my package of books and walked to the door of the shop. "See ya later!"

I stopped by the house and picked up the supplies I needed to do the rubbings at the cemetery on the stones I'd been unable to decipher. After changing into warmer clothes, I headed out toward the graveyard.

I made my way through the woods and soon found myself in the cemetery once again. I crept through the tombstones at a slower pace than before, but I could tell the evidence techs had been very efficient, as there was nothing more to be found.

I found the first of three tombstones I needed to take a rubbing of, so I set my messenger bag down and got to work. I held up the interfacing to get the proper height before cutting it to fit with my scissors. Then I used my masking tape to hold it securely in place on the tombstone. I withdrew my large black crayon from my bag and began to rub the stone, gently at first and increasing the pressure when the carvings on the stone began to show up on the interfacing. Once I was done, I removed the rubbing and carefully folded it before putting it in my bag. Then I repeated the process for the last two grave markers.

I stood up to stretch, saw the path the police had made through the woods and decided to follow it. Around me the forest was quiet and as I walked softly on the colorful carpet of the fallen leaves; the sound of a snapping twig caught my attention. I froze in place. What the hell was I thinking coming out here by myself? I darted behind a large oak tree and stood as still as possible. I could hear someone moving through the woods.

I crouched down and looked for anything I could use as a weapon. A large rock sat just out of my reach, and I had to crawl a foot or so to grab it before returning to my hiding place. I took a deep breath and peered around the tree. Not too far away, I saw the back of a man moving away from me. Even though most of the leaves on the underbrush were gone, it was still difficult to see through the twisted tangle of twigs and branches.

Using my cell phone, I snapped a picture, not that it would do much good. I cringed as the shutter clicked. As I watched, the man stopped, looked around, and pulled a gun out of his jacket pocket. Damn. The sound of my heart pounding echoed through my head, and I made myself as small as possible behind the tree.

As I watched, the man put his gun away and moved away at a slow, deliberate pace. I let out the breath I didn't realize I'd been holding and sat in place a few more minutes to make sure he didn't circle around and come up behind me. I got a brief glance at him when he'd turned his head but couldn't tell who it was. All I knew for sure was that he was wearing a dark coat, blue jeans, and hiking boots.

The voice in my head was screaming at me to get the hell out of there, but as usual, I chose to ignore it and cautiously came out of my hiding place and continued down the path. It'd been worn down by the army of police and other personnel that had traversed it to get to Lacey's body. About three hundred feet away I saw the flash of yellow police tape.

A few minutes later I arrived at the scene. The shallow grave that held Lacey's body was to my right under an oak tree. A pile of dirt sat to the left of the grave, and the ground was trampled down.

"Curiosity killed the cat," a male voice said from behind me.

I let out a squeal and turned around to see Jason Brock standing a few feet away from me.

"Sorry," he said and chuckled. "I didn't mean to scare you."

My heart was pounding, and I found it hard to catch my breath. I put out my hand and steadied myself against a tree. "Where did you come from?" I gasped.

"Over there," he said and pointed in the opposite direction I'd come from. "I got here and heard someone coming through the woods. I didn't know if it was the police or whoever killed Lacey, so I hid. Then I saw you."

"Why are you here?" I said. His coat and general build matched the man I saw a few minutes ago. It must have been Jason. But why was he carrying a gun?

He stuck his hands in his coat pockets and put his head down to avoid looking at me. "I'm kind of a true crime buff."

Or returning to the scene of the crime, I thought.

"Really?" I said and inched closer to the path out of there.

"Yeah, it's a hobby of mine," he said and shuffled his feet like a nervous teenager. "What are you doing out here?"

"I was finishing up my research in the cemetery and curiosity got the best of me." I moved farther away from him. "I should go, I have a lot of work to do."

"I'll walk you out." He moved closer to me. "You really shouldn't be out here by yourself. Something bad could happen to you." A cold chill ran the full length of my body.

"No need. I know the way. But I'm curious, how do you get here from the direction you came in?" I said and took a couple more steps backwards.

"There's an abandoned farm at the end of Ridge road. You just park there and the woods are behind the house. I work in the area and discovered it one day. I like exploring abandoned buildings, but I haven't been in that one yet."

"Another interesting hobby." I turned away and began to walk back down the path, stopping every few steps to make sure he wasn't following me.

When I got home, I fed Karma and pulled out the rubbings I'd made at the cemetery. I put an ironing mat on the kitchen table and plugged in the iron to let it heat up.

I took the first rubbing, carefully unfolded it and laid it on the mat, then I placed an old towel over it so the wax on the interfacing wouldn't get damaged. I picked up the iron and laid it on top of the rubbing holding it down in each spot for a minute or two to set the wax from the crayon. Once the first rubbing was completed, I repeated the process with the other two. I unplugged the iron to let it cool and took the rubbings into my office.

I was able to make out the names and dates, so I entered the information into my spreadsheet. I set the rubbings aside so I could give them to the historical society. The rubbings had come out perfectly, and I thought they might want to frame one or two of them.

As much as I tried to focus on researching the cemetery, I couldn't get my mind off Lacey's murder and Felix's death. With a sigh I set aside the cemetery research and pulled Felix's large rolling whiteboard out of the corner to the center of my office.

I printed out a picture of Felix and put it at the top right of the whiteboard. I did a search for Lacey Daniels and found a picture of her printed by our local newspaper in the article that announced her death. I printed out the picture and put it on the top left of the board.

Then I pulled out a stack of index cards and started to write down what I knew to be true – one fact per card – and put them next to the appropriate person. I remembered the list of the other girls Felix had on the SD card that'd been hidden in the book. After double-checking the names, and doing a few internet searches, I had pictures of Chloe Manning, Jenny Parker, and Lisa Conrad. I added them to the whiteboard.

After two hours of research, the details of each of their murders was added to the board. According to the newspaper articles I found, the primary crime scene in two of the murders hadn't been discovered yet. Chloe Manning's murder scene was discovered by a group of urban explorers who'd stumbled upon it while trespassing in a vacant warehouse. Now that must have been quite a shock.

The news article went on to say that there were candles, an altar, metal table with shackles, an old dagger and an old book.

Like Lacey, the other girls were thought to be runaways, and according to reports, were talking to someone online, but none of their friends or family seemed to know who, nor had they ever met the person they'd been talking to.

Without further details of how Lacey died, it wouldn't be easy to connect her death to those of the other girls, and I still didn't know if Felix's death had anything to do with Lacey's murder. After an hour or so, I sat back in my office chair and stared at the whiteboard. I knew this is what Felix was working on, and I needed his files. Felix had always kept meticulous notes.

I looked through the files Seth had dropped off, but the files pertaining to Lacey weren't there, nor for any of the other girls – if Felix ever had them. Damn that detective!

It was late afternoon by the time I made my way to the kitchen to feed Karma and get a soda. I was heading back to my office when the doorbell rang. It was Maddy coming to clean.

We greeted each other as she deposited her cleaning supplies in the foyer.

"I heard Lacey's funeral is set for Friday. Are you going?" she said.

"Yes, for sure." I headed back into my office so she could get to work.

She followed me and took her time studying the whiteboard.

"Interesting," she said, turning to face me. "So, you think the murders are related?"

"I'm not sure," I said and shrugged. "But Felix thought they may be."

I spent some time filling Maddy in on everything that had happened since we talked last. "Oh, you may not want to open the freezer," I added. "There's a box with a dead bird in it."

"In the freezer?" She wrinkled her nose at me.

I chuckled. "Yes, sent by my secret stalker."

"It's not funny, Zoey! You could be in real danger," she said, giving me a stern look.

"Maybe," I said. "But I refuse to be a victim and I have to find out what happened to Felix."

"Who are your suspects?" she said, shaking her head and turning back to the board.

"It's too early to say, but right now one of my suspects is Jason Brock. I know next to nothing about him. He's kind of quiet. I find him attractive, but his eyes are intense."

"In what way?"

"I'm not really sure how to describe it," I said and hesitated. "It's like when he looks at you, his eyes bore into you. It makes me uncomfortable, but in a sexy kind of way. His hair is curly and long – well, just above his shoulders, anyway. He's built like a tank, you know? Like he works out."

"Yeah, that's not contradictory at all, Zoey," she said and laughed. "But, seriously, do you think he had anything to do with Lacey's murder?"

"It's possible," I said, taking a sip of my soda. "And he could be the one who's sending me all those texts and the dead bird. I mean, he just lives across the street."

"He does? Well, that puts him at the top of my list," Maddy said. "Who else?"

"Henry Daniels told me that Lacey's friends said she met someone online before she disappeared." I wrote the word "Suspects" on the board and put Jason Brock's name underneath it. "Henry said that he didn't know anything about her talking to someone, and that her friends said the guy's name was Robert, and he was older, but they'd never met him."

"Hmmm," Maddy said. "I'd definitely add him to the list."

I agreed and wrote the name "Robert" down on the board underneath Jason.

We both stood back satisfied with the board as it was.

"I'm going to be awhile, if you want to go get some dinner at Gil's while I clean," Maddy said. She didn't like people underfoot when she was working.

I hadn't eaten since breakfast, so I didn't put up a fight. I put on my coat, grabbed my bag, and headed out the front door. The walk into town might do me some good.

As I walked, I thought about the abandoned house Jason mentioned when I saw him in the cemetery that morning. I put it on the top of my "to do" list for the morning.

By the time I'd finished eating, and done some window shopping in town, it was getting late. When I got home, Maddy was gone, so I let myself in and went to bed.

CHAPTER NINE

I woke up determined to check out the abandoned farmhouse Jason had told me about. I spent the better part of the morning completing some work for my clients and by early afternoon I found myself once again heading in the direction of the old cemetery.

I drove north out of town and turned right on Ridge Road that ended at the woods. Where the hell was the farmhouse? As I peered out my windshield, I saw a two-track driveway to my left. Judging by the way the weeds were bent and broken, someone had been down there recently.

Now I had a problem. Do I drive my Jeep to the farmhouse which would be about as stealthy as a train wreck, or do I walk in? I opted to walk. I looked around and saw a golf club down the road to my right. I parked in their parking lot, grabbed my bag, and headed into the woods.

I stayed just inside the tree line alongside of the driveway and within a few minutes the house came into view through the branches of the trees. I crouched behind some underbrush and scoped it out.

There didn't appear to be any vehicles there, but I couldn't see the back of the house to be sure.

The old Victorian house looked like something out of a Gothic horror movie. The outside of the house had weathered to a dark grey. Cobwebs hung from the wood covering the windows, and the unkempt undergrowth and ivy growing up the walls made the house appear as if it had sprouted out of the ground.

A barn stood toward the rear of the property, and while not in good condition, seemed to be withstanding the test of time.

I left the safety of the woods and walked toward the house. I was mesmerized by the home's beauty and in my mind's eye, I could picture it fully restored. I made my way around the outside of the home looking for a way in. At the back of the house I found a loose board on one of the windows but couldn't pull it off enough to gain access.

"Boy, you really came prepared for this excursion, didn't you, Zoey," I said as I looked around for something to give me leverage. I found a thick branch and wedged it between the wood and the house, but it snapped in two when I applied a lot of pressure. Damn it!

The barn! I ran across the yard and forced one of the old barn doors open enough to squeeze through. The barn smelled musty, and I caught a whiff of rotting hay. I pulled my flashlight out of my bag and could see old stalls and a large loft. A layer of old hay lined the floors.

I noticed a small room at the back, so I headed in that direction. Old leather harnesses still hung on rusty hooks, and various animal brushes were on a rotting workbench. Must have been the tack room, I thought, as I explored further. Something glinted in the light, and I saw old farrier tools hanging on the back wall of the room. I grabbed a large rasp and darted back out of the barn, careful to shut the door behind me.

Returning to the loose board, I slid the rasp in behind the wood and pushed hard. I could feel the board starting to give way. It took some time, but the board finally popped off with a gruesome creak and landed on the ground. The window behind it was open, which struck me as strange, but I didn't question my good fortune.

Not wasting any time, I hoisted myself through the window and started to explore. I found myself in what I guessed to be an old parlor. The flashlight revealed a large fireplace to my left, a door to a hallway on my right, and a large opening in front of me that led to another room. The stillness of the house was deafening. The wide-plank hardwood floors looked to be original and were worn and smooth.

The rotting corpses of dead mice, birds, and insects littered the floor and made a sick crunching sound as I made my way across the room. The curtains that hung at the windows were limp and moth riddled.

A few pieces of old furniture protected by dust-covered sheets sat in the center of the room.

I decided to go straight and noticed the original pocket doors used to separate the rooms were still slid into the walls. I grabbed one and pulled. The door protested at being moved after all these years but acquiesced and slid forward to reveal its beauty. They were intricately carved, and the mahogany finish looked pristine; they had survived the years of abandonment protected from the elements by being hidden in the wall.

I left the parlor and walked into a large foyer which had a set of stairs leading to the second floor. Across the foyer I found a dining room that opened into a kitchen that'd seen better days and was probably last renovated in the 1940s. A large powder room was by the back door.

Old radiators were everywhere and cast eerie shadows on the walls when the light hit them. More than once the shadows caused me to jump back and run for cover. Oh my God, get a hold of yourself, Zoe.

Stairs to the basement and the back door were off the kitchen, but I decided to go to the second floor. I tested each step for soundness as I made my way up the stairs. There were four large bedrooms with fireplaces, and two bathrooms, but none of the rooms looked like anyone had been in them for many years. I trudged back down the stairs and wound through the rooms on the first floor to the basement stairs.

When my light hit the steps, I saw that the thick layer of dust that covered just about every surface of the house had been disturbed. You could see footprints where someone had walked down the stairs not too long ago. Question was: when?

I crept down the stairs one at a time, stopping every other step to listen for anyone moving around in the basement. I made it to the bottom and was faced with many options. There was a long hallway straight ahead of me with doorways on both sides, a room to my immediate left, and a room to my right.

The room to the right of the staircase was lined with shelves of dust-covered ceramic molds. Mouse droppings trailed across the floor and shelves. Old rodent-chewed bags of cement sat on the floor, and a wood-burning kiln was in the far corner. I wanted to spend hours looking at the molds, but I knew I'd already been in the house too long.

The room to the left of the staircase must have been a workroom. Decrepit wooden workbenches sat against the far wall, and a dank, musty smell permeated every square inch of the space. Tools with wooden handles hung on hooks above the workspace.

Each room that lined the hallway was the same; small and empty.

As I approached the room at the end of the hallway, the musty smell of the basement was replaced by an almost sweet, but sickening smell. It took me a second to place, it, but I realized it was the smell of death. My heart skipped a beat and my nerves felt as if they were on fire.

I stood in the doorway and shone the flashlight around the large room. Pedestals holding red, burnt candles sat at the four corners of a metal table. Shackles had been welded onto the table at each corner and looked like they were covered in dry blood. If Lacey was here, she must have been terrified. Fighting off the urge to vomit, I tore my eyes away from the gruesome scene and played the flashlight around the room. It landed on a make-shift altar not too far from the door. As much as I wanted to go into the room for a closer look, I didn't want to disturb anything in case Lacey was murdered here.

I snapped a few pictures with my cell phone and enlarged the picture of the altar to see if I could make out more detail.

A wooden pentagram stood at the back of the altar and black, red, and white candles surrounded a large book, but I couldn't see it clearly.

I turned to call the police, but in the same moment, I heard someone moving around on the first floor. My pulse was racing as I ran back to the room with the ceramic molds and hid behind one of the crowded shelves. I turned off the flashlight and said a silent prayer that I wouldn't be discovered.

As much as I wanted to call Seth, I knew I couldn't because the light from my cell phone would give away my location. You should have called him before you even climbed through the window. What the hell is wrong with you? I admonished myself. Now look at the predicament you've gotten yourself into.

As I stood in the darkness, I could hear my heart pounding in my ears and little else. I forced myself to make it slow down long enough to hear what was going on in the house.

I could hear someone walking toward the basement stairs. Heavy footfalls hit each step and every agonizing second felt like an eternity. I peeked out between the mold of a gargoyle and urn-shaped planter and saw the shadow of a man just outside the door. The light from his flashlight revealed he was holding a weapon straight out in front of him - like a cop. Seth?

But what if it wasn't? Was it worth revealing my location? Taking a deep breath, I eased out from behind the shelf careful not to disturb anything and tip-toed across the room staying in the shadows as much as possible. I took another step forward and heard a mouse skeleton crunch under my foot.

The man whirled around and as he did, I screamed.

"Zoey!" Seth yelled and lowered his weapon. "Jesus, I could have killed you! What in blue blazes are you doing here?"

"It's a long story," I said, trying to catch my breath. "I think Lacey was killed here. Follow me!" I turned on my flashlight and headed down the hallway with Seth hot on my heels. I stopped just outside the room and stood aside so he could see into the space.

He illuminated the room with his flashlight and stood in stunned silence absorbing the scene that lay before him. I couldn't really blame him, it'd shocked me as well.

"Son of a bitch," he whispered.

"My thoughts exactly," I said and went to stand next to him.

He reached into his coat pocket for his cell phone and dialed a number. After a short conversation, he hung up and looked at me. "Come on, let's get out of here until the cavalry arrives."

I nodded. I'd had enough exploring for one day.

Seth took my arm and led me up the stairs. Neither one of us spoke as we made our way back into the fall sunshine. He helped me get through the window and I collapsed on the ground. He sat down next to me.

"Explain," he said.

I told him about my encounter with Jason and learning about the farmhouse. "Fair is fair, what are you doing here?" I said.

"Dispatch got a call from the golf club saying they'd seen a woman go into the woods. They were concerned, given what happened to Lacey. The description matched yours and it sounded like something you would do, so I took the call to keep you out of jail," he said. "You're really becoming a pain in the ass, Zoey."

"I'm just trying to find enough evidence to get you to reopen my uncle's case. If you'd do your job, maybe, just maybe, I wouldn't have to do it for you," I said and got to my feet. Without looking back, I walked to the front of the house. Seth followed.

"Zoey," he said and ran his hands through his hair. "I have to follow the law and certain procedures. Right now, I don't have enough to justify it."

I whirled around to face him. I clutched my hands into tight fists at my side. "What do you need? Tell me! Do you need someone else to die? Do you need my stalker, who is probably the killer, to murder me? Would that be enough for you?"

"That's not fair!" His angry eyes met mine.

"No, it's not! Do you know what else is not fair?" I bent down and picked up my bag. "What's not fair is my uncle was murdered, and you refuse to investigate it!"

Before he could respond, a small army of police personnel pulled up to the house with a small garrison of equipment. I watched as one of the policeman walked up to the front porch and used a pair of bolt cutters on the padlock that secured the front door. Within seconds they were in the house.

Before long, two generators were running, bright lights on stands illuminated the entire house, and the crime techs were in the murder room in the basement.

Seth was busy in the house and I didn't want to be in the way, so I made myself comfortable on one of the porch steps. My mind was trying to wrap itself around the macabre scene in the basement. The ping of my cell phone jarred me out of my thoughts. I pulled it out of my pocket and saw a text from my stalker. It said: "Be careful. I'm watching you."

CHAPTER TEN

It took everything I had not to react – I wouldn't give this creep the satisfaction. I got up and walked back into the house. At least with all the policemen crawling around the place I'd be safe.

Seth was standing outside the room leaning against the wall. The grim look on his face told me this wasn't the time to tell him about the text. I put my phone in my pocket and stood next to him.

"Who owns this place?" I said.

"I don't know. Someone at the station is working on it," he said, turning to look at me. "Do you think someone at Dixon's Bookstore could tell me about the book the killer left?"

"What book is it?" I said.

He walked into the room and picked up the evidence bag that contained the book and then handed it to me.

"The *Lessor Key of Solomon*. Interesting," I said, reading the cover through the plastic bag.

"You know about it?" he said,

"Yes. The first section is the Ars Goetia. The ritual in this section is said to be able to summon seventy-two demons, but not just any demons. The Ars Goetia summons seventy-two specific demons, and it's been said that King Solomon evoked and sealed them in a bronze box. While it's widely believed that the demons can't be used to do someone's dirty work, the demons can be excommunicated," I said, looking up at him.

"How the hell do you know all this?" he said.

"I collect rare books, and I like the paranormal and metaphysics," I said.

"Is there more?"

"The Ars Goetia also contains holy magic which is supposed to allow the user to get the Gods of Hell to sign an oath that gives the user power over Hell and help the person using the book discover true and sacred wisdom using magic squares."

"What does all that mean? Am I looking for a Satanist?" he asked, brushing his fingers through his hair.

"Maybe," I said, handing the book back to him. "The other items on the altar would suggest that's what this was about. I don't remember the Ars Goetia having anything to do with human sacrifice."

"I want you to stay out of this right now, it's police business."

"But..."

"Just stay out of this!" he said through clenched teeth.

"I can't do that, Seth." I hung my head. "Lacey's murder may have something to do with Felix's death and until you make the connection, I'm all in."

"I'll put it this way. If you don't stay out of this, I'll arrest you for interfering in a police investigation for your own good," he said, his voice low and threatening.

"You call it interfering; I call it assisting. You wouldn't have found this place if it wasn't for me," I said, my tone matching his. "Good day, Detective."

I walked away from him and wound my way out of the house and started through the woods back to my Jeep.

A short distance away I heard something moving through the woods to my left. Holy crap! I'm a damn idiot. I knew my stalker was out here!

I picked up my pace, keeping an eye open for anyone. I could hear him keeping up with me, but I couldn't see anyone through the thick underbrush and right now I was too pissed at Seth to even care.

I emerged from the woods and broke into a fast trot until I reached the parking lot of the golf course. I kept looking back over my shoulder to see if someone else came out of the woods, but no one appeared. I jumped into my truck and hightailed it back to the house.

After sharing some tuna salad with Karma, I grabbed my cell phone and went into my office to download the pictures I'd taken of the crime scene. Karma followed and made herself comfortable on my desk while I waited for my computer to boot up.

I pulled up the pictures and examined each one closely before printing it out and putting it on the whiteboard. The similarities between Lacey's murder scene and Chloe Manning's were obvious.

Turning my attention back to my computer, after a bit of research, I confirmed the Ars Goetia doesn't include human sacrifice. Hmmm, was Lacey sacrificed? If so, why?

Setting it aside for the time being, I turned my attention back to the cemetery project for the historical society.

It only took a couple of minutes to find out the abandoned house was owned by the city. The pedigree of the house went back to the mid-1800s and was originally built by the Rockman family. It made sense, considering the Rockman's also owned the land the old cemetery was on.

I looked at my watch, 4 p.m., the museum would still be open. I printed out my preliminary report and got ready to walk the short distance into town.

When I got to the museum, the door was unlocked, so I walked through the door, wound my way through the gift shop and found Pam Davis and Jason Brock sitting at the dining table. I noticed Jason had some mud and leaf debris on his hiking boots. Perhaps he went for a walk through the woods?

They both looked up when I walked in, and Jason gave me a broad smile.

"I came by to give you an update on the research I'm doing," I said as I took off my coat and hung it on the back of a dining room chair. I sat down by Pam.

"Oh? Already?" Pam said as she tucked a wisp of shoulder-length grey hair behind her ear. She turned to look at me, her bleary blue eyes locked on my face.

"Yes," I said, opening my file. "Preliminary research is showing that this could be the witch cemetery; some of the tombstones belong to the women on the list you gave me, the ones accused of being witches."

Jason's eyes were sparkling. "How cool is that?"

"It is cool, but that's not all," I said. "The others buried in the cemetery are from the Rockman family. Were you able to find anything out about them?" I looked at Jason. Before he could speak, Pam chimed in.

"Oh yes!" Pam said. "They were one of those rich families in town back in the mid-1800s. After old man Rockman and his wife died, their children seemed to disappear. The town's rumor mill still yaps about them." She rolled her eyes.

"Really? What are the rumors?" I took out my cell phone and laid it on the table to record the conversation.

Pam looked nervously at the phone. "Do you really have to record this? You know how I am," she said and laughed.

"Yes, I want to make sure I get my facts straight. Even though these are just rumors, there's usually a grain of truth to some of them."

"Okay," she said, her shoulders collapsed in defeat. "Well, the main rumor, and probably the one closest to the truth, is that one of the Rockman's, a nephew named George, I believe, got into some trouble. Some say he killed someone; others say he wrote bad checks. Anyway, the other rumor is that David Rockman, the one who built the house, was having an affair with one of the barmaids at Herman's Bar. Others believe he was frequenting a brothel that used to be where the bakery is now."

"Interesting," I said. "Where was Herman's Bar?"

"Where Christie's funeral home is now," Jason said. "Where they are building the new storefronts, and apartments around the corner on Main Street."

"Oh, by St. Agatha's Our Grace Community Center," I said, forming a map in my head.

"Exactly!" Jason said.

"What do you think happened to the Rockman's, Jason?"

Jason sat back in his chair and looked over at me. "I'm not sure," he said, measuring his words. "I'm more inclined to believe that George was up to no good. I found old newspaper articles last night saying he was somewhat of a troublemaker. I know his first wife divorced him on the grounds of extreme cruelty. But that wouldn't be enough to make the family leave town, would it?" He looked at me.

I shrugged. "Depends on what kind of trouble he got into, I suppose."

"It could be the rumors about David Rockman are true. Who knows?"

"But David died, and there isn't a George Rockman buried in that cemetery, at least there wasn't a tombstone with his name on it," I said, turning off the recorder on my cell phone and putting it in my bag. "David Rockman's wife is buried there, but I haven't confirmed the family relationships between the other Rockman's yet."

"Maybe you can crack this little mystery!" Pam said.

I smiled at her and gathered my things to leave. After saying good-bye, I took my time walking back home.

I found Seth on my front porch waiting for me. What the hell?! He was the last person I wanted to see. Wordlessly, I walked past him and let myself into the house. He followed. I put my bag on the kitchen table and grabbed a couple of sodas out of the refrigerator.

"Look," he said, as he sat down at the table. "I'm sorry about earlier."

"But …?" I said, joining him. I wasn't ready to let him off the hook yet.

"I need you to stay out of this. I know you think Lacey's murder and your uncle's death may be related, but you've got to let me handle it. Okay?" he said and drained the soda bottle in three gulps.

"It's a little late for that, don't you think?" I said, taking the empty bottle he held out to me and walking to the kitchen sink.

"No, it's not too late. I can't investigate Lacey's murder and keep you safe at the same time," he said. "If you keep poking around, whoever murdered Lacey could make you his next victim. I don't want that to happen."

He stood uncomfortably close to me while I rinsed out the soda bottles at the sink. I breathed in the scent of him, woodsy, earthy.

I turned to face him. "Oh, wait, you're one of those men with a knight in shining armor complex, aren't you?"

"I am not," he said, a little too fast. "It's my job to protect the citizens of Hope Harbor."

"If you say so," I said, hiding a smile.

Karma had made her way into the kitchen and jumped onto the kitchen table. Seth reached out to pet her, and she nuzzled into his hand and started to purr.

I opened the freezer and pulled out the box with the dead bird in it. "So, can you protect me from the person who did this?" I gingerly placed the box in front of him and sat down at the table.

He gently lowered Karma to the floor and opened the box. His eyes went wide when he saw the dead bird, and a grim look spread across his face.

"When did you get this?" he said, looking at me.

"It was on my front porch a couple nights ago."

"Why didn't you call me?" he said, his voice filled with anger.

"So, you could do what, exactly? I'm over being scared. All he's doing now is pissing me off."

He put the lid back on the box and stood up. "A little dose of fear can be healthy. Sometimes it can keep you alive."

Without another word he walked out the front door, shutting it behind him. I stood in the kitchen, looking after him with my mouth hanging open.

I finished up some work and sent it to my clients before going to bed.

CHAPTER ELEVEN

The next morning, I woke up early so I could take my time getting ready for Lacey's funeral. I poured my coffee and wandered around the house looking at everything with a critical eye.

I'd received the life insurance check two days ago and had dumped it into my savings account, but there were rooms in the house that needed updating. I decided to have the carpet on the first floor taken out and hardwood floors put in their place and update the kitchen and bathroom. I was pretty sure the house hadn't been updated since the late seventies and it was long overdue.

I decided to walk to St. Agatha's instead of driving, so I didn't have to try to find a parking spot close to the church. As I approached the church, I saw throngs of people milling around and talking in small groups before heading inside.

It appeared that, just as at Felix's funeral, the entire town had shown up to pay their respects to Lacey. I saw Henry and his wife Jill walk up the stairs to the church. Henry seemed to be holding Jill up. Her face was ashen, and her eyes vacant. My heart hurt for her.

Jax and Seth were standing off to the side watching the people as they filed in for the services. I saw Jason Brock and Pam Davison go inside and decided to head in myself. The breeze from the lake was blowing my hair out of place and making me shiver.

As I made my way toward the stairs, I saw Agent Phillips, the FBI agent I did work for, walking up the sidewalk. His eyes caught mine, and he gave me a barely perceptible nod. I smiled at him and continued into the vestibule.

Just as I was starting to walk into the sanctuary, my cell phone pinged. I moved out of the line of people and pulled my phone out of my purse. The text was from Agent Phillips. It said, "Go into a confessional after the service."

As I found my seat in the sanctuary, I noticed a confessional in the back left corner. Lacey's funeral was probably the saddest funeral I'd ever attended. Such a young life taken in such a senseless manner. As hard as he tried, even the priest had a difficult time explaining how God could let something like this happen. By the time the service ended, there wasn't a dry eye in the place.

The mourners started to file out and go to the church community center for the wake. Given the number of people who attended, that was the only building that could possibly accommodate so many people.

I ducked into the confessional and a minute or so later, Agent Phillips slid into the priest's side.

"I was sorry to hear about your uncle," he said. "Are you okay?"

"Thank you, I'm fine," I said, adjusting the curtain to make sure it was shut all the way.

"I've heard you've been getting threats. You need to stop looking into Lacey's death," he said. "It's too dangerous. Tell me what's happened."

I told him about all the texts and the dead bird, along with my suspicions surrounding Felix's death, and the other information I'd been able to learn.

"I think all the deaths are due to a serial killer," I said.

"It appears that way," he said, shuffling around in the tiny booth. "Now do you understand how much danger you're in?"

"Yes, but I need the case files from the other murders."

I heard him sigh. "I can't give those to you, you know that. Just stay out of this and lay low for a while. Give me some time to gather more evidence. I think I'm close to making an arrest. Trust no one, Zoey. If you receive any more threats, text me."

"Deal," I said, gathering my purse and gloves. I slipped out of the confessional, made my way out of the church, and headed in the direction of the community center, Agent Phillips' words still ringing in my ears.

Jason Brock fell into step alongside of me. "Where were you? I looked for you after the service."

"I had to freshen up. What did you want?" I said, glancing at him. I had to admit he cleaned up well. His curly hair was pulled back, and he looked extremely handsome in his black suit.

He took my elbow as we came to the curb to cross the street. "I was just curious whether you'd learned anything else about the witch's cemetery or the Rockman's?"

We crossed the street and followed the other people up the sidewalk to the center.

"Not yet, but I plan on working on it this weekend. I'll let you know. Hey, do you happen to know a good contractor? I want to get some work done in the house."

"Yeah, actually I do. I'll text you his number later," he said.

"Thanks." I saw Maddy a few feet ahead of me and gently eased my arm out of Jason's grip. "Talk to you later, Jason. I have to go meet my friend."

I increased my pace to catch up with Maddy and we hugged our greeting.

"What was up with that?" Maddy said, nodding in Jason's direction.

"Work stuff," I said and sighed.

It was early afternoon by the time I managed to extricate myself from the wake and head home. I felt overwhelmed and confused by my conversation with Agent Phillips.

I let myself into the house and after changing into a jogging suit, I got into my Jeep and headed to a home center to look at kitchen cabinets, flooring, and everything else I would need.

Two hours later I left with a ton of pamphlets, flooring samples, and paint chips. I drove through a taco place on the way home. I had to admit I was feeling better – retail therapy had that effect on me.

While shopping, I'd ignored all the pinging of my phone and it wasn't until I got back home that I even bothered to look at it.

There was a text from Jason with the name and number of a contractor and another one from my stalker which read: "You looked very pretty today. What did you have to confess?"

I felt as if all the blood had rushed out of my body, and I struggled to remember all the people I'd seen at the church today – an impossible task. One thing I was pretty sure of; the serial killer had attended his victim's funeral. The very thought made me nauseous. Agent Phillips might have had a point – maybe I should lay low for a couple of days. Yeah, like that was going to happen. I chuckled as I settled at the kitchen table with my tacos.

After eating, I called the contractor Jason told me about, and he agreed to come by the house in about an hour. While I waited, I went into my office and turned the whiteboard around so all the information on it was facing the wall.

As I walked to the bathroom to make sure I was presentable, I took a detour into Felix's bedroom. Maybe it was time I moved downstairs, I thought, but I'd need a new bedroom set. The idea of sleeping in Felix's bed just didn't seem right to me.

The doorbell rang, so I ran to greet the contractor, Dustin Proctor. We walked through the house and talked about what I wanted to do. He also came up with some great ideas I never thought of. Despite being about my age, he seemed to be very knowledgeable and experienced. He said he'd work up a quote and get back to me in a couple of days. After he left, I considered getting a couple more quotes, but I liked Dustin and felt comfortable with him.

Knowing I couldn't put off the inevitable, I went back into my office, switched the whiteboard back where I could see it and worked on a couple of small jobs for my clients.

As I researched the cemetery, the disappearance of George Rockman nagged at me almost as much as Lacey's murder. I spent the better part of the day digging for information about him, but other than the information Jason had found, there was little more to be learned.

Before bed, I'd found his birth certificate, but all the deceased George Rockman's I could find weren't a match for the one I was looking for. What the hell happened to him?

CHAPTER TWELVE

The alarm went off annoyingly early the next morning, but I got up, threw on sweats and let myself out of the house for my morning run. I stopped at the bakery on the way home to get a cup of coffee to go and walked the rest of the way home to let my muscles cool down.

I locked the front door and walked down the hall to my office. Karma followed me and jumped into the box that held the items of Felix's the police had returned. She looked up at me and mewed.

"What?" I said, shooing her out of the box.

Sitting at the bottom of the box was Felix's laptop. Hmm, I wonder… I pulled the laptop out and made room on my desk to set it down. After plugging in the charger, I turned it on and waited for it to boot up.

There was nothing on it. It had been reset to the factory settings. Did the police do this? Maybe Felix did. If he felt he was being threatened, it's possible. Then something in my mind clicked, and I remembered the disks that I'd found in the file cabinet. They'd said, "recovery disks," written in Felix's hand. Maybe?

I leapt out of my chair and pulled open the bottom file drawer. After a little digging around, I found them.

Within a couple of minutes, I had the disks in Felix's computer and uploading files. The anticipation was killing me, and I tried to distract myself by working on some client jobs.

After what seemed like an eternity, the files were uploaded, and I started to explore Felix's laptop.

I opened the document folder and various sub-folders popped up on the screen. There was a folder for Lacey and each of the other missing girls. Now I was getting somewhere! I clicked on Lacey's' folder. It was empty! Same with the folders for the other girls! What the hell!

Felix was meticulous. He wrote reams - stream-of-consciousness stuff - it was the way he sifted through his ideas… he had to write down his thoughts. There's no way he wouldn't have any notes associated with these cases. Where the hell were they? Had Uncle Felix destroyed them because he felt threatened?

I hit the picture folder and discovered they were the pictures Felix had taken at the park, which I already had.

The "Notes" folder looked interesting, and I clicked on it to open it. Almost the entire folder consisted of pictures. What's up with that?

As I clicked on them one by one, I realized they were pictures of threatening texts and notes. The only document in the folder was a list of the dates and times of the threats, and the activity he'd been doing just before receiving them. So, he was being threatened too! Holy crap!

I went back through the pictures of the texts Felix had taken of his phone noting the telephone numbers. Like the ones I'd been receiving, each number was different, but the message was clear – stay out of the Lacey Daniels case.

Every time a text was sent, Felix had been out talking to people, scouting different locations, or hanging around the park at night, according to his notes.

I printed out all the pictures and the document, cut them to size, and added them to the board under Felix's picture.

Another document called "Loans" caught my eye, and when I opened it, there was a spreadsheet with people's names, the amount of money Felix loaned them, and how much they had paid back. Now this was going to be interesting! The more I'd thought about it, the more it made sense that Felix would want to help out his friends if he could.

I recognized most of the names on the list; Danny Lewis, Abby, and Jason Brock. Danny Lewis had been making regular payments, and his balance was next to nothing. Jason also made payments, but not on a regular basis and the amount he'd borrowed from Felix was negligible. Abby, Felix's next-door neighbor was another story, she owed Felix well over five thousand dollars and as far as I could tell, hadn't even attempted to pay him back. What the hell?

I shook my head as I printed out the spreadsheet, and moved onto another file called, "Inventory." It was also a spreadsheet with a list of items Felix owned at the time he made the list. I'd noticed many of them when Mom and I had cleaned out the house, but many items on the list hadn't shown up yet. Probably for the house insurance company, but where's the rest of the stuff? The last time the file was modified was a day before his death.

Most of the items on the list were clothes and some household items, but there was also an entry for a small file box. I looked around the office, but there was only the large, four-drawer cabinet, and I know my mother and I hadn't found one when we were going through Felix's things.

Something in the back of my mind clicked, and I remembered seeing a small lockbox at the bottom of Felix's closet when I was here visiting one weekend. I ran to his bedroom and flung open the closet doors. The lockbox was gone but I could see the indentation in the carpet where it'd once sat. Did the police take it, or did Felix's killer take it when they left?

I couldn't worry about it now. I had to get back to the old cemetery, and I wanted to take another peek at the Rockman house.

After feeding Karma and getting showered, I packed up my messenger bag and headed out.

After a quick stop at the hardware store for a small pry bar, I drove out of town. I pulled down the two-track dirt driveway to the house. No more parking at the golf club for me. The last thing I wanted was for Seth to find out I was here. I parked behind the barn and walked through the overgrown grass to the house.

The wood covering the window was no match for the pry bar and it only took a few seconds to get into the house. I set the wood back in place over the window and clicked on my flashlight.

Everything on the first floor appeared to be unchanged, so I made my way down the stairs to the basement. I walked down the hallway towards the room Lacey had been murdered in. My flashlight picked up the yellow police tape that'd been used to block the room off. It'd been ripped away and hung like two limp flags from the door frame. Who did this? The police?

My body started to tingle, and my palms started to sweat. Was I alone? I didn't even think to check. Damn it!

I turned off my flashlight and stood perfectly still – listening for any movement in the house. Everything seemed quiet, so I turned my flashlight back on and peered into the room.

Most of the items had been removed. All that remained was the metal table and the tall candle holders. I could see a single set of footprints in the thin layer of dust and dirt on the floor. That's weird. I would think there would be a lot of footprints due to the amount of police traffic that'd descended on the room a few days ago. Unless they swept the floor clean to look for evidence and the dust had settled.

I shone my light on the footprints and snapped a couple of pictures with my cell phone. Judging by the prints, my thought was they'd been made by a man, but I couldn't be sure. To me, the tread appeared to be made by a type of boot, maybe a hiking boot, but it'd be impossible to know for sure until I did some research.

My mind jumped back to the debris that'd been on Jason's hiking boots when I saw him at the museum. Could he be the one that'd been in here? He did say he liked to explore abandoned buildings. Hmm.

I went back down the hallway to the room with all the ceramic molds in it and took my time investigating every nook and cranny. I had no idea what I was looking for, but the pull to return to the house had been too strong to ignore. There must be something here I missed before.

I trudged up the basement stairs and did a cursory search of the first floor before heading upstairs to the bedrooms. As I walked around the bedroom that would have probably been the master, my eye caught something on the top shelf of the closet. It looked like a book.

Being only five feet tall has its disadvantages, and this was one of them. While I could reach the edge of the closet shelf, the book had been pushed to the back. I pulled the pry bar out of my bag and used it to bring the book closer to me. Finally, I was successful, and I had it in my hands.

The large rectangular book was covered in dust and smelled musty and moldy. It must have been in the closet for years. I blew some of the dust off and wiped the outside of the book with my hand.

It appeared to be an old ledger book, but when I opened it, I saw, written in a woman's hand, the genealogy of the Rockman family. The last date a new entry was made was in the late 1800s.

I thumbed through the pages and saw whoever wrote this also used it as a kind of diary, noting family events and their thoughts about what was going on in their life. I felt like I'd struck gold.

As much as I wanted to sit down and read the whole book, I knew I'd already been in the house too long, so I tucked it in my messenger bag and headed down the long hallway toward the stairs.

I was almost to the stairway when I heard a loud crack. I stopped in my tracks. Before I could even assess the situation, the floor gave way, and I felt myself falling.

CHAPTER THIRTEEN

I landed hard on a dirt floor and lay there writhing in pain. The entire left side of my body hurt. Panic overwhelmed me and I began to cry and yell for help. Idiot! No one can hear you scream out here. Stop it! Calm down!

I took a few ragged breaths and struggled to sit up. I tested every part of my body; other than an excruciating headache and injured left ankle I seemed to be in good shape.

Where the hell was I? I crawled around and found my flashlight. When I hit the button, the light revealed I was in a small room. I played the light around until it landed on a human skeleton laying on a low cement bench against the back wall.

I let out a scream and turned the light away from the gruesome scene. Gathering what little courage I had left, I crawled over to where the skeleton was and took a closer look. Even though the clothes were tattered and rotting, it didn't take long to realize they were from the 1800s. The beam of my flashlight hit something shiny. It was a gold chain, a watch fob. I could see the pocket watch under the skeleton and eased my hand under the rib bones, all the time trying not to gag.

I looked at it under the light and, when I opened it, saw the name "George Rockman" engraved inside. I was almost giddy with excitement – I'd found him! My excitement turned to horror. So many questions about how and why he'd ended up in here flooded my mind. I had to force myself to concentrate so I wouldn't suffer the same fate. I had to get out of here!

After inspecting every square inch of the room, I discovered that I was underground. Three of the walls were made of old cinder block and there was a wall made of wood on the far side of the room. I sat down and thought about the layout of the house. I'd been near the stairs when I fell, and below that was the basement, but there were block walls between the rooms in the hallway of the basement. I must be in one of those spaces between rooms, but how the hell do I get out of here?

Using the cement bench, I managed to stand up. The flashlight revealed three dilapidated wooden stairs that led to a wall of wood. Maybe a door?

I tried everything I could think of to get it open, but nothing worked. After a little searching I found my messenger bag and pulled out the pry bar. I wedged it between two of the boards, but I didn't have enough strength or the proper balance to get the boards loose.

Frustrated, I sat down on the bench to catch my breath and to get the pain in my body under control. I had to get help, and fast. I pulled my cell phone out of my bag, praying that I could get a signal. I dialed Jax's number.

"Zoey! What's up? Long time no—"

"Jax! Shut up and listen to me!" I was met with silence.

"I'm at the Rockman house. I fell through the floor and am trapped in a secret room. I think I broke my ankle. Please, help me." By the time I had finished telling Jax what happened, I was in tears. I was starting to sweat, and I felt dizzy.

"On the way, Zoey. Sit tight." Like I had a choice. The line went dead.

The dizziness began to overwhelm me, and I felt myself sliding off the bench.

I woke up lying on the floor, and it took me a minute to remember where I was. I could hear Seth and Jax screaming my name.

"I'm here!" I said, crawling onto the cement bench.

I heard their footsteps thundering down the hallway.

"Stand back, Zoey!" I heard Seth yell.

I was as far back as I could get but I put my arms over my face and turned my head away from the door. Seconds later wood splintered and flew through the air, to shower down on me. Seth and Jax scrambled through the door towards me.

"Where are you hurt?" Seth said and knelt down in front of me. Jax sat down beside me.

"My ankle … and I hurt everywhere. I think I passed out," I said through tears of pain.

"It's going to be okay," Seth said, and made a call on his cell phone.

Jax played his light around the room and saw the skeleton. "Oh my God."

"It's George Rockman," I said, taking a couple of ragged breaths.

"Who?" Seth said.

"Long story." I put my head on Jax's shoulder and he put his arm around me.

Minutes later, emergency medical personnel showed up, stabilized my ankle, and strapped me to a board. As they were carrying me out of the room, I realized I'd been in a room beneath the stairs leading to the second floor. The storage closet under the stairs contained a hidden door to the room. Hmm.

"My bag, and there was a book. Please, Jax," I said as I was loaded into the ambulance.

"Got it. I'll see you at the hospital," Jax said.

"I'll check up on you later. I have to deal with the skeleton you found," Seth said.

It turned out I had only sprained my left ankle and suffered a concussion. It took Jax's promise to the doctor that I wouldn't be left alone to get the hospital to release me.

Two hours later Jax was helping me up the front stairs to my house. I'd never been so happy to be home in my life. After feeding Karma and making sure I was settled in on the couch, Jax headed back out to pick up my prescriptions at the drug store.

As soon as Jax left, I called my mom and put her on speaker because it hurt my head too much having the phone close to my ear. I told her what had happened and asked her to come stay with me for a couple of days. Before she could answer, Seth walked into the house and I motioned for him to be quiet.

"I knew no good would come from you moving out, and I warned you to stay out of things that are none of your business," she said, her words slightly slurred. Was she drunk already? "No, I'm not changing my plans to come take care of you. Maybe you'll learn something from this."

"But Mom..." I said. I could feel tears welling up inside me.

"I'm sorry, but you made your bed, Zoey, now you're going to have to lie in it," she said, and the line went dead.

I sat and stared at the phone, speechless, until Seth took it from my hand and put it on the coffee table. "Is there anything I can do?"

"Yes," I said, wiping my eyes on the edge of the blanket that Jax had put over me. "You can tell me about the skeleton."

"You probably know more than I do at this point," Seth said and headed into the kitchen. "Do you want anything?"

"A soda, please."

"The skeleton is at the coroner's office. He's going to try to confirm identity, but the watch pretty much spells it out."

Seth brought me a soda and an ice pack for my ankle. He gently removed the walking boot cast the doctor had put me in and placed my foot on a throw pillow. He then put the ice pack on my extremely swollen ankle.

While he busied himself doing that, I told him about the Rockman family and my inability to find George Rockman.

"Interesting. Do you know if there are any living relatives we could do a DNA test on just to confirm?"

"No, not right now. Maybe my research will turn up someone," I said and shrugged.

"Let me know, but I'll tell the coroner what you told me. Maybe he can figure something out. I brought your car home," he said, dropping my keys on the coffee table.

Jax came back into the house and Seth filled him in on the skeleton.

"I have to get to work," Jax said. "You call me if you need anything."

"I will. Thanks, Jax."

When Jax left, Seth sat down in the chair by the couch. "You know I should read you the riot act for being in that house."

"I know. It was stupid. I should have never gone there by myself," I said.

"Just don't do anything like that again, okay?" he said. He tried to be stern, but the smile he was trying to hide gave him away.

"Promise," I said.

Seth got up to leave. "Are you going to be okay? Can I call someone?"

"I'll be fine. Thanks again for rescuing me," I said.

He walked over to the couch and put his hand on my shoulder. "Any time. Let me know if there's anything you need, or if you find out anything about George Rockman."

"I will."

When Seth left, I put my removable walking cast back on and hobbled into the kitchen to get my messenger bag off the kitchen table. I'd just settled down on the couch to read the book when the doorbell rang. I sighed and sat the book down on the coffee table before answering the door.

"Zoey! Oh, my stars! What happened?" Bea Perkins said looking down at my leg.

Bea Perkins was a widow in her mid-60s who'd moved into the house next door a few months ago. I'd met her a few times when I'd been visiting Felix.

"I had a slight accident. It's fine really," I said, stepping back to let her enter.

"I brought you some soup and a piece of apple pie. I saw a handsome young man helping you up the porch a bit ago," she said, brushing past me and heading for the kitchen.

"Thank you," I said, following her.

"What in blue blazes do you think you're doing? Go sit down and put your foot up this instant," she said, ushering me to the couch.

One thing I'd learned about Bea in the short time I'd known her is that you don't argue with her when she tells you to do something, you just do it.

I sighed and got into a half-sitting, half-laying down position. Bea fussed with a pillow to get my ankle elevated and went back into the kitchen.

"How are you holding up after Felix's death?" she said. I could hear the clattering of dishes in the kitchen.

"I'm okay. I miss him terribly," I said as I stared longingly at the old book lying on the table in front of me.

Bea brought in a bowl of the soup she'd made and handed it to me. She sat down in one of the chairs in the living room.

"Such goings on in town lately," she said and sighed. Her brow furrowed in worry. "What with Felix's death and now Lacey Daniels being murdered. It's like the devil himself has paid Hope Harbor a visit."

"Yes, it's been a bad few weeks," I mumbled between bites of the delicious dinner.

Bea and I chatted while I ate and she filled me in on the church gossip - about who was doing what, and who was getting divorced, married, or ill.

When I finished my dinner, Bea took my bowl and washed it out in the sink.

"There's a nice piece of apple pie on the counter for you to have later. I have to get home and tend to Atlas," she said, gathering her purse and the dish she'd brought the food over on.

"Give Atlas a hug for me," I said, remembering that Atlas was the huge German Shepherd her and her husband Johnny had gotten a few months before Johnny died of a heart attack.

"I will. Call if you need anything," Bea said as she walked out the front door.

I got up and locked the door before grabbing the book from the Rockman house and settling back on the couch.

It didn't take long to learn that the journal had been written by Mrs. Rockman. She'd written about her husband's indiscretions at Herman's Bar, and more importantly, she wrote about the antics George was up to, writing bad checks and abusing his first wife. She even said she believed he had burned down the hotel he built in town just to get the insurance money. She was disgusted by his behavior, and several times mentioned how she wished he would just go away. Interesting.

On several pages she'd penned what I thought were poems, but then I realized they were spells. So, she had practiced witchcraft! I wondered if she'd been friends with some of the other women accused of witchcraft, and that's why they all were buried on what was, at the time, land owned by the Rockman's. Well, this put a new spin on things.

As I read through the spells, I realized they were recipes and incantations to cure certain illnesses, and to either help or harm someone. Is that considered witchcraft? Seemed like a fine line to me.

I fell asleep reading the journal, and when I woke it was almost dark. My ankle was throbbing, so I got up, took a pain pill and turned on some lights. Before heading to my office, I shut the blinds, and grabbed something to eat. It was after 2 a.m. before I hobbled my way upstairs to bed.

CHAPTER FOURTEEN

I normally love Saturdays, but this one was shaping up to be bad. When I woke, my ankle was killing me, and I had to scoot down the stairs on my butt, because I didn't trust myself not to fall down the stairs. Just another reason why I should redo Felix's room and move downstairs.

After starting coffee and feeding Karma, I took a pain pill and grabbed an ice pack for my ankle. I opened the bottom drawer of my desk to prop my foot on and started playing catch up with my emails.

Dustin had sent the quote for the remodel and I emailed him back and asked when he could start. He replied immediately that he'd start the middle of the week and for me to clear out everything as much as possible. Great. That should be interesting with my ankle.

I texted Maddy, told her what had happened and offered to pay her extra to come over and help me pack up all the stuff, and get rid of the furniture. She agreed, and we planned to get together that afternoon. That meant I had to get to the grocery store for food, snacks, and wine.

Showering and getting dressed took longer than expected because of my ankle. I slung my messenger bag over my shoulder and drove to a supercenter to shop.

Thankfully, I could hang onto the shopping cart for balance, and took my time wandering through the store. It was early Sunday morning, and the store wasn't crowded. I picked up some cat food and kitty litter before heading toward the back of the store to get to the grocery section.

As I got to the electronic section, I paused to pick up some ink for my printer and happened to look down one of the aisles. I saw Jason Brock standing in the pre-paid phone section. He had two or three phones in his hand! What the hell?

I ducked behind an endcap so he wouldn't see me, grabbed my cell phone out of my bag, and snapped a couple pictures of him. This caused me to get some weird looks from a couple of other shoppers, but I didn't care.

Glancing around, I grabbed my cart and disappeared into the women's clothing section. The high racks of clothes allowed me to keep out of sight as I wound my way through the store. Jason had to be my stalker! I felt so rattled, I had to stop and collect myself before quickly getting what food I needed and getting out of there.

When I got home, Jax and Seth were waiting for me on the porch and brought in the groceries for me. They even offered to hang around and take out what furniture I didn't want any more because garbage day was the next day.

"I think Jason Brock is my stalker," I told them as I sat down at the kitchen table and put my ankle up on a spare chair. Jax got me an ice pack for my ankle and finished helping Seth put away the groceries.

"Why do you think that?" Seth said and sat down at the table.

"I saw him at the store this morning buying multiple burner phones. I got a picture," I said as I adjusted the ice pack on my ankle. "My stalker is using a different burner phone each time he contacts me. And Jason lives right across the street."

"Maybe," Jax said, "I'll cruise by a few times tonight to make sure you're okay."

"I'll check into him and see what I can find out," Seth said. "What furniture is going out to the road?"

"All of it," I said and chuckled. "Just leave the kitchen table and the recliner. I need something to sit on."

Maddy showed up a few minutes later, and she helped me pack up the kitchen and bathroom except for things I would need during the renovation. I ordered a couple of pizzas late in the afternoon, and after eating, Jax left for his shift, and Maddy went home.

"Any luck on George Rockman?" Seth said as he cleaned up the kitchen.

"Not yet. I probably won't get to it tonight. I'm pretty tired and my ankle hurts." I hobbled into the living room to sit in the recliner and put my legs up. "Can you get me a pain pill? They're on the counter and a glass of water?"

"I need to get back," he said, handing me a pain pill and glass of water.

I put the pill in my mouth and chased it down with the water. "Thanks for all your help today."

"Anytime. Call me if you need anything." He then disappeared into the night.

I woke up the next morning still in the recliner. Those pain meds must have really kicked my butt. I got up and made coffee. Maybe it was time to get to know Jason a little better before jumping to conclusions. After all, it wasn't a crime to buy burner phones.

After pouring my coffee, I peeked out the front blinds and saw Jason's truck in his driveway. I texted him and told him I had some exciting news about the Rockman's and asked him to come over.

He texted back and said if I made the coffee, he'd go get cinnamon rolls at the bakery. Deal.

When Jason got to my house, I had to explain to him what happened to my ankle and about finding George Rockman's skeleton in the hidden room.

"Glad you're okay, but wow!" He sat back in the kitchen chair, speechless.

"I know, right?" I said, taking a bite of my cinnamon roll.

"So, George was murdered?" he said, sipping his coffee.

"Maybe," I said and shrugged. "It's a great place to hide a body. And if he knew that room was there, which he probably did, then I can't think of any reason he'd go down there willingly, can you?

"No," he said, shaking his head. "And another mystery that may never be solved involving that family."

I nodded in agreement. "What do you think the room was used for?"

"I don't know. The underground railroad, maybe? I mean the house is old enough," he said, his eyes gleaming at the possibilities.

"That would be cool," I said. "But that's not even the exciting part."

"There's more?" he said and got up to get us more coffee.

"Look at this!" I said and slid the large journal across the table to him.

I sat back and watched his emotions wash across his face as he read the journal, his eyes growing wide. Eventually, his dark brows furrowed, and his jaw dropped open.

"This is amazing!" he said a while later as he laid the book on the table.

"It really is."

We spent most of the day going through the journal page by page, discussing every detail, every possibility. Around three o'clock, I started to make us a late lunch, but he stopped me, and made me go sit with an ice pack while he made us some soup and sandwiches.

It was after 8 p.m. before we called it a day. As I watched him walk across the street, I let out a dreamy sigh. He was so handsome and easy to talk to. He made me feel comfortable and we could laugh together. Put the brakes on, Zoe. Damn it! He's a dangerous man! Most serial killers are charming and smooth, like Jason. That's how they attract their victims.

CHAPTER FIFTEEN

I changed into my pajamas and tidied up the kitchen before settling down to watch the news. Just as I turned on the television, I was greeted with a breaking news report with an amber alert. Ashley Montague, a teenager from Richland, was reported missing. My blood ran cold. Richland is only fifteen miles away from Hope Harbor.

The station switched to a reporter at the girl's house; the distraught mother was saying that they didn't believe she ran away, and she wasn't having any problems at home. Yeah, right. She's a teenage girl, there's always problems at home, but I couldn't blame the family for not wanting to air any issues they might be having on television.

Apparently, she'd been at a friend's house and left to go home but had never arrived. She was last seen walking past the waterfront at around ten-thirty. Hmm, well that takes Jason out of the equation, he'd been with me most of the evening. No, wait, he'd left between eight and eight-thirty; that gave him plenty of time to get to Richland. I peered out through the front blinds and saw that Jason's truck wasn't in his driveway.

My whole body started to tremble, and I was sweating. I felt hot and cold at the same time. I hobbled into the kitchen and poured myself a large glass of wine before going into my office to study the whiteboard.

The Rockman house! That's got to be where he'd take her. There still might be time! I scrambled upstairs as fast as my ankle would let me and threw on a pair of jeans and a sweatshirt. I thumped down the stairs into Felix's room. I'd put his gun on the shelf of his closet, and I checked to make sure it was loaded before tucking it into my messenger bag. A loud thunderclap and lightening greeted me as I walked out the door to my vehicle. As I headed down the street, the skies opened up and rain pelted my windshield.

Speed limit be damned! I drove as fast as I dared out of town and turned down the driveway of the Rockman house, turning off my lights half-way so as not to alert anyone I was there. Someone turned in behind me!

I stopped my Jeep just short of the end of the driveway. I leapt out of my truck, the gun at my side.

Whoever was behind me got out of their pickup, the lights from the vehicle illuminating the weapon in my hand.

"What the hell are you doing? Put that gun down!" a man said, taking a step towards me. The headlights revealed it was Jason.

"Where's Ashley?" I said, tightening my grip on my gun.

"Zoey, I…" he said

"Put your hands up!"

He put his hands in the air and when he did, I saw he was wearing a shoulder holster.

"I'm an…" he said.

"Be quiet!" I said. I walked around his truck and looked in the back of the pickup. It was empty; so was the cab.

I walked back in front of him and I saw him start to reach into his jacket pocket.

"Stop!" I could feel my hands shaking as I pointed the gun at him.

"Reach into my jacket pocket. My wallet's in there," he said.

I kept the gun trained on him and my body as far away from him as possible as I stuck out my hand and pulled his wallet out of his pocket. I flipped it open to see an FBI badge with his name on it.

"See? We're wasting time. Stay here!" he said.

"I thought you worked construction," I said, lowering my gun. FBI? But what about the burner phones? I turned to say something, but he was already gone. I could barely make out his silhouette as he crept closer to the house.

Stay here? Screw that! I tucked the gun into my jacket pocket and grabbed my cell phone before I began to follow him, crouching down to stay low. My ankle was slowing me down and, by the time I got to the back window of the house, I was soaked to the skin. Jason had already disappeared inside.

I hoisted myself through the window and turned on the flashlight app on my phone. I had the layout pretty much memorized by now, so it took me no time to get to the basement stairs.

I peeked down the stairs and could see the beam from Jason's flashlight playing around the different rooms in the basement.

"Jason?" I whispered rather loudly.

"They're not here," he said, appearing at the bottom of the stairs. "It doesn't look like anyone's been here."

"Damn it!" I said and walked into the kitchen. I heard Jason coming up the basement stairs.

From the kitchen I went out into the hallway and opened the closet under the stairs. What was left of the door to the hidden room gave way with a gentle push and I shone my light around just to make sure it was empty. I heard Jason walking around the second floor and then coming back down the stairs.

We stood in the large foyer looking at each other, neither of us ready to admit defeat. The silence in the house was deafening. The ping from my cell phone caused me to jump, and I saw Jason hide a smile.

It was a text from my stalker: "Nice try."

A small scream escaped my lips. Jason grabbed my phone and read the text.

"Son of a… Let's get out of here," he said, handing me back my phone and putting a protective arm around me. He led me to the window, climbed out, and then helped me get out of the house.

We walked the rest of the way back to our vehicles in silence, the earthy smell of the rain-soaked forest filling our nostrils. "Meet me at your house," he said, opening my car door for me.

I nodded and got into my Jeep. I pulled into my driveway a few minutes later. Once in the house I grabbed a large bath towel and dried off as best I could. I grabbed a spare one for Jason. I expected to see him right behind me, but it was another ten minutes before he pulled his truck into his driveway. I saw him crossing the street with carry out bags from my favorite taco restaurant and opened the front door for him.

We settled in at the kitchen table.

"Tell me everything," he said, using the towel to dry himself off.

As we ate, I told him everything from the moment I got the phone call telling me Uncle Felix was dead, up to what had happened that night. He listened intently and didn't even interrupt me, even though I think I was rambling a bit.

When I had finished, he sat back in his chair and closed his eyes as he processed the information.

"Show me the board," he said, getting out of his chair and clearing the table.

We walked into my office and he spent some time studying the whiteboard with all the information I'd assembled.

"This is good," he said. "Well, except the part about me being your main suspect. How long do you think he's keeping them alive?"

I shrugged. "I'm not sure. A day, maybe two."

"That would be my guess. The problem is, I'm not working these cases; another agent is."

"Agent Phillips," I said and nodded.

"How do you know?"

"I do some work for him. We had a little meeting at Lacey's funeral. Are you two in the same office?"

Jason nodded. "I requested a transfer from the D.C. office to the Detroit office and have only been here about six months."

"Why did you want to transfer?" I said, settling into my desk chair.

"I started to do the family's genealogy," he said, his face turning a little red. "I found out they were from here and visited last summer. I really liked the small-town feel, so put in my transfer request."

"I see," I said. I didn't quite buy it, but I couldn't disprove it either.

"Then I wandered into the museum one day, and the rest, as they say, is history. Pardon the pun." He shrugged.

"Interesting," I said and giggled. "But Pam Davis told me you worked in construction?

"I'm undercover. Shh," he said, putting his index finger to his lips.

"Gotcha," I said, pursing my lips together and pretending to lock them with a key.

"I'm going to talk to Agent Phillips and ask him to look into your uncle's death."

"Why?" I said and searched his face for answers.

"Because I'm worried about you and that stalker. I'm convinced it's the same person who killed Lacey and now has Ashley," he said, and I saw him set his jaw. "I don't want you to be next."

"Thanks," I said and gave him a hug.

"There's nothing more we can do tonight. Let's talk in the morning. It's late."

I glanced at the clock. It was after midnight.

After Jason left, I walked back into my office and put a question mark next to his name on the board. I wasn't ready to cross him off my suspect list so quickly. It was still possible he had an accomplice. Agent Phillip's words, "trust no one" echoed in my head.

Karma sat at the door to my office hunched down getting ready to launch another cat zooming antic. As I got out of my chair, she launched herself into my office and onto my desk, sending everything but my laptop and printer onto the floor. Pens and pencils rolled across the room. "Bad Karma!" I said as she zoomed past me and into the living room. I picked up the debris and replaced everything on my desk.

Before heading up to bed, I went to put Felix's gun back in his closet but thought better of it and took it upstairs with me.

I woke up early, showered, and got dressed. Dustin was supposed to start renovations today, and I didn't want to answer the door in my pajamas. I turned the whiteboard in my office towards the wall and settled in at the kitchen table to have my morning coffee.

A soft knock at the door jarred me out of my thoughts. I opened the door and Jason strode in with cinnamon rolls from the bakery.

"I talked to Agent Phillips this morning," he said, sitting down at the table next to me. "We're getting agents and local police together to check out all the abandoned buildings in the area to try to find Ashley."

"It's already too late," I said, looking over at him. "Ashley's dead. The text he sent me last night when we were at the house told me that."

"Meaning?" he said, leaning back in his chair and looking at me.

"Meaning, he's not stupid. He had to know the Rockman house would be the first place we'd look. Even if he'd been there, he wasn't going to wait around for us to find him. If she wasn't dead when he texted me, then he killed her shortly afterwards. He knows the police are going to be checking all the abandoned buildings. The only logical move he had was to kill her and dispose of the body."

"Maybe, but I'm not giving up hope," he said, getting out of his chair.

"I really hope you find her alive," I said, putting my hand on his arm. "Let me know."

"I will. Stay safe," he said. "Oh, by the way, Agent Phillips said he'd look into Felix's death." He winked at me and walked out the door.

I quickly cleaned up the kitchen and by the time I'd finished, Dustin and his crew arrived to start demolition. After making sure they understood the scope of work, I took Karma and went into my office to get some work done.

As hard as I tried to concentrate on the tasks at hand, my mind kept wandering to the events of the previous night. Something still didn't sit right with me.

There'd been no one around when we'd come out of the house, and our cars were hidden by the woods making it impossible to see from the road. So, how did my stalker know I was there? I know I hadn't been followed by anyone. But just because you're FBI doesn't automatically exempt you from being a cold-blooded killer, and his explanation, while plausible, seemed a little lame to me.

I'd taken Jason's word there was no one in the basement, but I hadn't checked it out myself. I'm an idiot! After putting Karma's food, water, and litter box in my office, I closed the door, shutting her in.

As I walked to my car, I saw Bea Perkins attempting to walk her German Shepherd, Atlas. However, it appeared to me that Atlas was walking her.

When he saw me, he broke away from Bea and raced towards me. I braced myself for impact. Atlas stopped just short of hitting me and put his front paws on my shoulders, licking my face.

"Oh Zoey, I'm so sorry," Bea said, rushing up the sidewalk as fast as her legs would carry her.

"He's fine. Are you okay?" I'd noticed she was limping. Bea was an older, heavy-set woman, and I worried about her.

"It's my knees – arthritis," Bea said and sighed. "I just can't get Atlas out as much as I'd like to anymore. He has all this energy, and with me working at the church, he's alone a lot during the day."

An idea popped into my head. "Bea, would it be okay if I took Atlas for a while this morning? I have some research at an old cemetery in the middle of nowhere. It would give Atlas a chance to run, and I'd feel safer having him with me." Well, the last part wasn't a lie.

"Oh, he'd love that! Thank you, Zoey. I have to leave for work. Do you want me to give you a key so you can put him back in the house?" Bea said, breaking out in a big smile. I knew the dog was too much for her, but it'd been her husband Johnny's dog, and she didn't have the heart to get rid of him when Johnny died.

"No, he can hang out with Karma and me today. See you later!" I said and gave her a quick kiss on the cheek. "Come on, Atlas."

He willingly jumped into the passenger seat of my Jeep and we headed out of town together, with him happily hanging his head out the open window.

I pulled halfway down the driveway of the Rockman house and stopped. I put the gun in my jacket pocket and grabbed Atlas' leash before letting him out of the car.

After a few corrections, Atlas was walking with me, and not pulling me down the driveway. It took twice as long as it should have to reach the house as Atlas had to stop and smell what seemed like every blade of grass.

When we got to the back window, I noticed that either Jason hadn't replaced the wood, or someone else had been here after we'd left. The thought caused my whole body to quiver.

I opened the window and let Atlas off his leash. With a little urging, he finally jumped through the window into the house.

"Wait, Atlas," I said, as I climbed through the window. This walking boot was becoming a pain in the ass, and I couldn't wait to get rid of it.

By the time I got into the house, Atlas was gone, and I could hear his nails clicking on the hardwood floors as he ran around the bedrooms upstairs. So much for stealth.

"Atlas, come here!" I said in a loud whisper at the bottom of the staircase.

He came bounding down the stairs, his tongue hanging out, and his tail wagging a hundred miles an hour. I couldn't help but laugh.

"Let's go," I said, walking towards the basement stairs.

Atlas ran down the croaky steps and began exploring every nook and cranny. I didn't call him back to me, because if there was someone down here, he'd flush them out rather efficiently.

I walked through the basement at a more leisurely pace, partly because I wanted to look around, but mostly because the stupid boot on my foot wouldn't allow me to move much faster.

There was no one here. Everything looked exactly like it did the last time I was here. So, Jason hadn't been lying last night. I took out my cell phone and texted Agent Phillips to see if indeed he'd talked to Jason. He texted back and told me he had talked to him this morning – just like Jason said he had … unless they were in this together. Could Agent Phillips be Jason's accomplice? I shook my head. Now I was just being paranoid.

I trudged back upstairs with Atlas on my heels. I climbed back through the window and called to the dog who followed me out. I shut the window but left the wood off, just like I'd found it.

As I walked back to the car, Atlas was running around like crazy, so I decided to walk back over to the cemetery. I left the dog off leash so he could run freely and burn off some of his energy.

Atlas ran back and forth across the path, stopping only to sniff an interesting smell, but I noticed he never strayed too far from me and would look back occasionally to see where I was.

We emerged into the clearing and after my research, the cemetery seemed to take on new meaning to me. I felt as if I'd known some of the people buried there.

At first, Atlas stayed right by me, unsure of the tombstones and his surroundings. Then he saw a squirrel, and the chase was on. I yelled for him several times, but he ignored me. I could hear him thrashing through the underbrush, and then all went quiet.

I headed in the direction he'd gone and then heard him barking excitedly. What the hell? Did he tree the squirrel? I quickened my pace, and, by the time I caught up to him, he was pawing at the ground frantically. I could see leaves flying everywhere.

I grabbed his collar and pulled him away. I made him sit and told him to stay. When I was satisfied that he was going to listen, I went over to where he'd been.

Bits of white flesh stood out against the scattered dead leaves. Was that a body? I bent down and carefully brushed away a few more of the leaves with my hand revealing a head with long hair – blonde hair! Oh my God, it had to be Ashley.

CHAPTER SIXTEEN

I stifled a scream and plopped down on the ground. Atlas came over to me and nuzzled my face with his nose. I wrapped my arms around his neck and took a couple of deep breaths to calm myself down.

I put Atlas on his leash and got to my feet. Keeping him on a short lead, I examined the scene. I don't see any shovel marks. Was she buried in a hurry? I looked around and saw patches of bare ground, as if someone had swiped up all the leaves and moved them.

Kneeling back down by the body, I swiped away a few of the leaves. Ah ha! It was a natural depression. The sides of the makeshift grave were smooth and covered with a thin layer of grass.

I led Atlas to the edge of the cemetery and dialed Seth's number. He sounded distracted. "Zoey, I'm a little busy right now."

"I found Ashley. She'd dead," I said.

"What?"

"She's buried by the cemetery not far from where Lacey was. I'm at the cemetery now," I said, heading in that direction.

"We're on the way." The line went dead.

I sat down in the cemetery and leaned against a large tree. Atlas lay down next to me and put his head in my lap. I wanted to call Jason, but should I? I sat and stared at my cell phone. Oh, what the hell, it would be interesting to see his reaction. I dialed his number and filled him in.

"Sit tight," he said.

About fifteen minutes later, Jason and Seth burst onto the scene followed by a small army of policemen and evidence techs.

Jason crouched down next to me. "Tell me what happened."

"Atlas found her. She's about twenty yards that way," I said and pointed. "He disturbed the scene."

"Don't worry about that," he said, helping me to my feet.

Seth, who'd listened to our conversation, walked up to me. "You okay?" he said, putting his hand on my arm. "Can you show me where she is?"

"I'm fine," I said. "She's this way."

"What made you come out here this morning?" he said, as we started to walk in the direction of Ashley's body.

"I had more work to do in the cemetery. I brought my neighbor's dog with me. He was running around. The rest you know," I said.

Seth nodded.

"She's over there," I said and pointed.

Seth headed toward the grave. "Thanks. Why don't you go home? We'll talk later." Jason took Atlas' leash and let me lean against him as we walked back to my truck.

"Are you going to be okay? I really need to stay here until Agent Phillips arrives," he said.

I took the leash from his hand and put Atlas in the truck. I got behind the wheel and scrambled for my keys. "I'm fine. Talk to you later." The truth was I really just wanted to be alone. I needed time to think.

I got home to find the kitchen gutted; Dustin and his workmen were just starting to remove all the carpet on the first floor.

"We're going to do the bathroom after we finish the kitchen," Dustin said. "I didn't want to leave you without any water on the first floor."

"Thanks!" I could have hugged him. Obviously, I hadn't completely thought the project through and was grateful he had.

Atlas gave the workmen a rowdy greeting, and I walked back to my office to check on Karma. She was sitting in her spot on my desk, looking out the window, and mewed loudly when she saw Atlas. After ten minutes of hissing and Atlas getting swatted on the nose a few times, they both settled down. Atlas lay down on the rug and Karma fled to the highest point of her cat tower that I'd moved into the office while construction was going on. After giving Atlas a bowl of water, I settled down at my desk.

I closed my eyes and tried to remember everything I could about the way Ashley was buried. Her hand was facing down, which suggested she'd been buried face down. I'd also noticed part of her naked shoulder exposed. Maybe she was naked or just partially clothed. I made a few notes so I wouldn't forget anything. A quick computer search yielded me a picture of Ashley which I printed out and added to the board. Under her picture I wrote in bullet list form what I knew about her disappearance and the discovery of her body.

"Hello?" Bea's voice pierced my thoughts.

I quickly turned the board toward the wall and opened the door to my office. Atlas bounded down the hallway to greet her.

"Back here, Bea!"

I heard her shuffling down the hallway and she appeared at my door. "Did Atlas behave?" she said, settling her ample frame into the overstuffed chair by my desk.

"He had a busy day," I said. I wasn't sure if I should tell her about the body.

"Someone came into the church and said they found the body of that poor girl from Richland today," she said, shaking her head sadly.

"Yes," I said and sighed. There wasn't going to be any way to keep this quiet so I might as well be the one to tell her. "Actually, it was Atlas who found her body."

Bea looked up at me, her green eyes opening wide. "He what?"

I told her about my excursion into the woods and how Atlas had dug up the body.

"Oh, my stars! All that training Johnny did really worked!" she said, calling Atlas over to her and giving him a hug. "Good boy!" she cooed.

"What training?"

"Oh, Johnny was training Atlas for search and rescue, and he'd started doing cadaver training with him right before he died. He ordered a bottle of that dead people scent. Lord have mercy that stuff stinks. He'd been working with Atlas since we got him. You know Atlas flunked out of the police canine training, right? He has a squirrel problem. He'd been training to be a cadaver dog. I laughed at him. How in the world could an old man like Johnny do search and rescue? He got winded just walking down the walk to get the mail," she said, and chuckled.

"Interesting," I said, leaning back in my chair. My mind was racing with possibilities. Perhaps I'd underestimated the big, goofy dog.

"Well, I got to get home and start supper. Come over and eat. See you in an hour," she said, standing up. "Come on, Atlas."

I watched them walk down the hallway, Atlas glued to Bea's side.

Dustin stood at my office door. "We're done for the day," he said.

"Huh? Okay," I said. I'd been so lost in thought I hadn't even heard him come down the hallway.

"We were prepping the floors, and I noticed a couple of loose floorboards. I'm going to need to fix those before we put in the new flooring, okay?" he said.

"Yes, of course. Thanks, Dustin," I said.

"No problem. See you in the morning. 'Bout eight."

I got changed and headed over to Bea's for dinner.

Over dinner we chatted about Atlas' training and Johnny, her deceased husband.

"That man," she said and chuckled. "When I was cleaning out his things, I found stuff hidden everywhere. Money in pockets, old lottery tickets."

"Really?" I said, pushing my plate away.

"Yes, it made me crazy," she said, looking around the room. "I'm still not sure I found everything. It seems like no matter what I open, there's something in it. Good lord, I can't even throw out a magazine without shaking all the pages out. I haven't had the courage to go through his tools yet. Lord only knows what will turn up there." She shook her head.

I laughed at her story, but I was distracted; a faded memory was trying to come to the surface. When I was about ten, I'd found some pretty rocks at the beach. I was so afraid my mom would get rid of them and I told Felix. He'd taken me into his bedroom and pulled up a couple of floorboards and put my rocks in there for safe keeping. He'd told me I could get them any time I wanted. Oh my God! The floorboards!

I quickly thanked Bea for dinner and rushed home. I ran into Felix's bedroom and after a few minutes, located the loose floorboards – they popped out easily. Nestled between the joists was a rectangular lockbox – the one that used to be in his closet.

I pulled it out and sat it on the floor. Underneath it was an old cigar box. I sat that on the floor and opened it first. Inside were the rocks and other treasures I'd found as a child. I could feel tears welling in my eyes; I wiped them away with the sleeve of my sweater. I couldn't believe he'd saved everything.

After putting everything back in the cigar box I set it aside and turned my attention to the lockbox. When I opened it, I found a stack of files, and as I flipped through them, I realized they were the case files for Lacey and the other girls.

I let out an excited yelp and did a happy dance around the empty room. Now I was getting somewhere! But how did he get these? Open case files generally aren't released to the public.

After putting the files back in the box, I took it and the cigar box into my office. I put the cigar box with my childhood treasures in the bottom drawer of the file cabinet and settled in at my desk to look through the case files. It was going to be a long night.

First, I wanted to look at the crime scene photos. I decided to start with Chloe Manning.

Just like Ashley, she'd been found face down in a shallow grave deep in the woods. I quickly scanned through the photos of the other girls; they were all buried the same way. After making a few notes on my board, I turned my attention back to Chloe's file. It was the only other murder in which the primary crime scene had been found. It might hold some valuable clues.

I scanned Chloe's photos into my computer and examined each one closely. From what I could tell, the crime scene was set up almost the same as Lacey's – the candles, the altar, even the same book.

After putting the crime scene photos up on the board, I began to focus on the autopsy reports to find the cause of death in each case.

First, Chloe, hmm, let's see. Ligature marks – from being shackled to the table most likely, needle mark in arm – only one. From the killer or self-inflicted? I turned to the toxicology report and discovered she had had a large amount of heroin in her system. Her eyes had been superglued shut, and she'd suffered repeated assaults before dying. Official cause of death was listed as an overdose of heroin. The death was ruled to be a homicide. I should hope so!

As I read Chloe's autopsy report, I felt nauseous and faint. I put the files back into the lockbox. I couldn't read any more tonight but had to make sure the files were safe. I put the lockbox back under the floorboards, reminding myself to retrieve them before Dustin came in the morning.

CHAPTER SEVENTEEN

I woke up early so I could go for my run before Dustin got here to work on the house. My ankle felt a lot better, and the swelling was gone. I tested it by jogging around the first floor. Excellent! I threw on my running clothes and headed out the door.

While I couldn't run my normal five miles, I managed a weak three, well, two and a half, as I walked the last half mile back to the house. Perhaps I overdid it just a tad. I limped back to the house around seven-thirty and retrieved the lockbox from its hiding place. I locked it in the bottom drawer of the file cabinet in my office and went upstairs to shower and get dressed.

At exactly eight o'clock Dustin knocked on the door and I let him and his workmen in the house. I'd set up my coffee maker in my office during construction and retreated there with Karma so the guys could get to work.

As much as I wanted to concentrate on the files of the girls, work orders had piled up and I had to take care of my clients. I gave up all hope of getting more work done by ten o'clock. The noise from the saws and hammering was making me jittery. I texted Maddy and asked her to meet me at Gil's for breakfast.

The tantalizing smell of bacon greeted me as I opened the door and I saw Jax, Seth, and Jason sitting together in one of the booths. What's up with that? The only empty seat in the place was the booth behind them. As I walked by them, we exchanged greetings and I slid into the booth and sat so I was facing the door. Maddy came in a few minutes later and she plopped down across from me. Her face was flushed, and she was breathless.

"Did you run here?" I said, after we'd exchanged greetings.

"Yes," she said, pulling off her gloves and tucking them in her purse.

The waitress appeared, and we both ordered coffee and breakfast.

"So, I heard they found Ashley's body," she said, dumping two creams into her coffee. "What is going on around here?"

"Yeah, I have a lot to tell you," I said, sitting back in the booth. I told her about finding Ashley's body, and finding the files of the other girls hidden in Felix's house, pausing only long enough to allow the waitress to deliver our food and refill our coffee cups.

"Oh my God," she said when I'd finished. "So, all the murders are by the same person?"

"I'm not sure yet," I said and shrugged. "I'm going to have Henry Daniels go to the medical examiner's office and try to get a copy of Lacey's autopsy file. Maybe then..."

"You're going to put him through that?" she said, her eyes growing wide.

"I know, but they won't give it to me, hell, they might not give it to Henry. It's still an open investigation. And I need Lacey's cell phone records," I said, pushing my plate to the side.

"You really should leave this alone," Maddy said, giving me a stern look. "The police are on it, I'm sure."

"I can't," I said, cupping my hands around my coffee mug. "Felix's death is connected to all of this, and I owe it to him to find out what happened."

"I understand," she said, reaching across the table putting her hand over mine. "Let me know what you need me to do."

"I hate to ask, and you can say no, but I really need some help going through the files of the other girls," I said, not even daring to look at her.

"I can do that. I'll stop and pick us up some dinner. Be careful, Zoey," she said, gathering up her things. She reached for the bill, but I snatched it away before she could get it.

"Thanks. You too."

When Maddy left, I called Henry Daniels and asked him to contact his cell phone carrier and get Lacey's cell phone records, including texts, for three months before her death. I asked him about the autopsy report, and he said he'd subpoena it if he had to.

I got back to the house and checked on the workmen. They were just starting to prep the floors to lay down the hardwood. Construction couldn't end soon enough for me. It'd only been a few days, and I was already over it.

As hard as I tried to get some work done, I felt restless and decided to go furniture shopping. After making sure the lockbox was secured in the file cabinet, I told the guys I'd be back soon, and left, glad to be able to escape to the quiet of my Jeep.

I loved to shop but found furniture shopping to be more difficult than I expected. I did manage to find a dark grey sectional with two contrasting chairs, a coffee table and two end tables for the living room, and a king-size bed and Mission style white headboard with matching pieces for what used to be Felix's bedroom. After I left the store, it dawned on me that a king bed might be a tad big for one person, but then again, I did share the bed with Karma and for such a small cat, she seemed to take up an extraordinary amount of room.

When I got home, I went into my office, shut the door, and forced myself to fill many of my client's orders. Some were simple skip tracing assignments which generally didn't take more than an hour or two, and many were background checks that took even less time.

Before I knew it, Dustin and his crew were leaving for the day. He walked me through what had been accomplished. The new flooring had been laid in Felix's bedroom, the hallway, living room, bedroom, and kitchen walls were painted a pale shade of grey. Things were starting to take shape.

Around six, Maddy texted and said she couldn't make it and apologized. I couldn't blame her—going through murder files is nothing short of torturous. The rumbling in my stomach reminded me I hadn't eaten since breakfast, so after feeding Karma, I threw on my coat, and started the walk to the Blue Bass.

I loved Gil's Diner, but the Blue Bass served alcohol, and I was in desperate need of an adult beverage. As usual, the restaurant was busy, and I squeezed into a small table at the front of the restaurant by the window that overlooked the street. I ordered a glass of wine and sat back to look at the menu.

After ordering, I sat back in my chair and gazed outside. There were people out and about. Some were walking their dogs, others just leisurely strolling down the sidewalks window shopping.

I saw a group of teenagers heading for the park and that gave me an idea. Maybe it was time to shift focus to the mysterious Robert that Lacey was talking to right before she disappeared, although I was pretty sure Robert wasn't his real name.

I called the pizza place on the boardwalk and ordered an extra-large pizza. After I finished my dinner, I picked up the pizza and walked across the street to the park.

As expected, the teenagers were gathered in the pavilion.

"Hey," I said putting the pizza down on the table. They looked at me and the pizza. "Help yourselves."

They all looked at each other before opening the box and taking a piece of hot pizza.

"Did you guys know Lacey Daniels?" I said, sitting down on the top of one of the picnic tables and putting my feet on the seat.

"Yeah," one of the boys said. "We went to school with her."

"I see. My name is Zoey, and her father has asked me to help find out what happened to her. I'm not a cop," I said, looking at each of them. Some of the kids ignored me, one or two shuffled their feet, and the others paid attention.

"Lacey was one of my best friends," a young girl said, walking over to me. She couldn't have been more than sixteen. Pretty, blonde. The killers type.

"You must miss her very much."

"I do. I'm Willow," she said, sitting down at the table and looking up at me.

"Nice to meet you, Willow. Her dad said he heard she'd been talking to someone named Robert. Is that right?"

"Yes, she met him online. I don't know anything about him. She usually told me everything," she said, shaking her head.

"But?"

"But every time I asked her about him, she changed the subject," she said, wiping a tear from her face with her fingers. I noticed her nails were bitten to the quick.

"I'm so sorry, Willow." I put a hand on her shoulder. "Do you know what chatroom she met this guy in?"

"There's a couple where a lot of us hang out and chat online," she said. "I can write them down for you."

"That would be great. Thanks." I retrieved a pen and piece of paper from my bag and handed it to her. She wrote a few lines and handed it back to me.

"Thanks," I said, tucking the items back into my bag. "Willow, stay out of the chat rooms and don't go anywhere alone until this guy's caught."

"I'm so scared," she said, wrapping her arms around her tiny body. "I saw on TV that they found the girl who was missing from Richland. Ashley, I think her name was."

"Yes." I got up from my seat and put my bag over my shoulder. "She looked like me, so did Lacey." Willow looked up at me, her eyes wide with fear. "In my criminal psychology class in school, we learned that serial killers have a type. Right?"

"Sometimes, yes." I didn't like where this conversation was going, but I refused to lie to her. What the hell were they teaching kids these days?

"I'm his type, right?" she said. "Light hair, kind of pretty, young."

"Just be careful. Don't go off with anyone you don't know, no matter who they are or what they tell you. Stay in a group, don't wander off alone."

In the light from the pavilion I could see her bottom lip quiver as she looked at me.

'Look, I'm not trying to scare you. I just want you to be safe, okay?" I said, putting my hands on her shoulders.

"Okay," she said, pasting a brave smile on her face.

We said good-bye and I started my walk home, the conversation with Willow replaying itself in my head. I'd probably be getting an angry call from a parent tomorrow wondering why I scared the crap out of their kid.

I sighed as I walked up the front porch steps and let myself in. I locked the door behind me and got the paper Willow had written on out of my bag. I poured myself a glass of wine and went into my office.

It didn't take long to set up a profile on one of the sites and get into the chatroom she'd told me about. I had no idea what teenagers talked about now, but it didn't take too long to realize they gossip about other kids, talk about clothes, their teachers, and other teenage angsts.

I sat back and watched the kids chatter. They changed subjects fast and seemed to have their own language filled with code words and slang. I made notes as I figured out what they were saying so I would be able to communicate with them without raising suspicion.

By midnight my brain was fried, so I exited chat, turned off my computer, and slowly made my way upstairs to bed. Karma curled up next to me and we soon were both sound asleep.

I jerked awake and sat up in bed, wiping my eyes as I fought through the fog of sleep. What woke me up? Maybe it was Karma. I reached out my hand and felt her next to me, sleeping soundly. I heard a noise downstairs. What the hell was that? Beads of sweat began to ooze out of my pores.

I leapt out of bed and tiptoed to the top of the stairs. Should I go down? The man probably had a gun, and I didn't have anything. Damn it, I had to find out! I heard footsteps. I think they were heading toward my office.

The walls began to close in on me as I eased myself down the staircase in the darkness. My heart was racing, but I forced myself to breathe calmly. I was going to need my wits about me if I was going to confront this guy. I fought to keep control even though I could feel my whole body shaking. Why the hell am I doing this? I should just call the police. Would they get here in time?

CHAPTER EIGHTEEN

When I got to the bottom of the stairs, I crouched down behind the banister trying to figure out what to do. I could hear my desk drawers being opened and closed, and the sound of the metal file cabinet as he tried to force the drawers open.

My eyes scanned the living room, and I saw the fireplace poker. As I tiptoed across the room, I could feel beads of sweat running down my back. As I reached for the poker, someone wrapped their arms around me from behind, pinning my arms against my body. I struggled to get free, and he slammed me, face first against the wall.

My head began to spin, and I felt as if I was going to faint. He smashed me against the wall again, hard, leaving me dazed. Before I could recover, he hurled me to the floor. I heard the front door being flung open. He was gone.

I lay on the floor for a few minutes trying to recover from the assault. My cheek and head hurt, and my ribs ached from his steel-like grip. I crawled over to the recliner and used it to help me get to my feet. Holding onto the walls in the hallway, I managed to make it to the bathroom.

It was too much. I collapsed on the floor and began to sob. Stop it! Get ahold of yourself, Zoe. I wiped my face on the sleeve of my pajamas, and when I looked, there was blood on the material. I was bleeding? I gingerly felt my face and head with my fingers, and at my hairline, I felt something sticky – blood.

I got to my feet and stumbled down the hallway to the kitchen table. I grabbed my cell phone and dialed Jason's number. It was only then I realized it was 3 a.m. He answered on the fourth ring.

"Zoey?" he said, his voice thick with sleep.

"A man…house…hurt." Those words were the only ones I could manage to squeak out before the line went dead.

In what seemed like mere seconds, Jason was at my side, leading me to the recliner. "Don't move," he said, and I saw him disappear. He came back with a wet washcloth and daubed my head. "I don't think you're going to need stitches. Band-aids?"

I pointed to a box marked "Bathroom" sitting on the floor in what used to be my kitchen.

He rooted through the box and came back with a bandage and antiseptic cream and he dressed the wound on my head.

I leaned back in the chair and closed my eyes. I heard him make a telephone call. A few minutes later, Jax walked into the house.

"Tell me what happened," Jax said, as he knelt in front of me.

I took a couple deep breaths before managing to get out my story. "I think he was after the files," I said, calmer now. "The files!"

I jumped out of the recliner, grabbed my keys out of my bag, and went into my office. While the office had been rifled through, things weren't a mess. My hands were shaking so badly I couldn't steady them enough to get the key into the lock. Jason took them from me and unlocked the file cabinet.

I opened the bottom drawer and took out the lockbox. The files were still there. I breathed a sigh of relief.

"What are those?" Jason said.

"The files of the other victims like Lacy," I said, replacing the lockbox in the drawer and locking the file cabinet.

"Where? How did you get those?" he said, his eyes hardened.

"Felix had them. I don't know where he got them," I said.

Jason and Jax followed me out of the office and back into the living room.

"I'm going to file a report and stay close to your house for the rest of my shift if I can," Jax said to me, then looked at Jason. "Are you staying here?"

"I plan on it," Jason told him.

"You don't have..." I started to say.

"I'm staying. Go back to bed," he said, his voice stern.

I was too tired to argue and got a blanket out of the front closet for him, before walking up the stairs to go back to bed.

When I woke up, Jason was dozing in the chair next to my bed, with Karma curled up on his chest, sleeping. I got out of bed and walked into the upstairs bathroom to survey the damage. The right side of my face was swollen, and I had a black eye – just peachy. My ribs hurt and when I lifted my pajama top up, I saw they were bruised as well.

I changed into my running clothes and put a blanket over Jason. I went downstairs to feed Karma, then headed out the door for my run. I was a half-mile in when Jason caught up to me.

"What in the hell do you think you're doing?" he said, as he slowed down to match my slower than usual stride.

"My run," I said, looking over at him.

He reached over and took my arm, forcing me to a stop. "Yeah, not today."

Normally I would protest being told what to do, but not this morning. My heart wasn't in it. We stopped on the way back and got a cup of coffee and breakfast to go at Gil's. We made it back just in time to let Dustin and his crew into the house.

Jason and I retreated to my office to eat breakfast and talk.

"And you didn't even get a glimpse of the guy that attacked you?" he said as he put some grape jelly on his toast.

"No. It was dark. He grabbed me from behind. It all happened so fast," I said, wracking my brain to remember any detail of last night's attack. "Something seemed familiar about him, but I don't know what it was."

We were interrupted by Seth. "The workmen let me in," he said, as he walked over to me. "Jax told me what happened."

"I'll be fine," I said. "But I appreciate you stopping by to check on me."

I got up and picked up the now empty carry out containers. As I walked out of the office to throw them away, I heard Seth and Jason talking, but couldn't make out what they were saying.

They both came out of the office and joined me in the living room saying they had to go to work. I thanked Jason for staying last night and after they left, I collapsed in the recliner. I knew I needed to get some work done and finish going through the files of the murdered women, but I felt exhausted.

The construction noise was doing nothing for my already aching head and I decided I was going to work in the quiet of the library. I unlocked my file cabinet to put copies of everything into their proper places, and my eyes rested on the lockbox that contained the files of the other murdered girls. I'd been so busy, I hadn't had time to look through them all, but too many people knew it was there. I had to come up with a better hiding place.

I emerged from my office, lockbox in my hands just in time to see the truck from the appliance store pull into the driveway. I alerted Dustin, and he said he'd take care of it. So, I ran up the stairs to my bedroom.

I'd noticed a large rectangular panel in my closet that went up to the attic. I'd never been up there, but no time like the present. I got the step stool that normally went in the kitchen, but I'd stored in my bedroom during construction and within seconds I was peering into pitch darkness. I got the flashlight out of my nightstand and tried again.

I could see various boxes and other items on the floor of the attic. I hoisted myself up to investigate. Someone had put boards on top of the joists, so it was easy to crawl around. After some searching, I found the perfect hiding place. I got to my knees and hoisted up the edge of one of the pieces of plywood and nestled the lockbox between two joists before replacing the wood.

I backed out of the attic and slid the panel back into place. After replacing the stool, I made sure there weren't any pieces of stray insulation on the floor.

When I went back downstairs, I packed up my laptop, locked Karma in my office with her food and litter box and walked to the library.

I set myself up at a table in the back that's partially hidden by bookshelves and dug into my growing list of unread emails. Two hours later I'd made a dent in the work for my clients, processed some payments, and moved the money into my checking and savings accounts.

Satisfied with my progress, I sat back in my chair and stretched. The cemetery project was taking longer than I expected, but I'd managed to accumulate most of the information on the women buried there by early afternoon.

Now I just had the Rockman's to contend with. I tried to concentrate on the task at hand, but my mind kept wandering to the events of last night. Obviously, whoever it was wanted the files on the other girls, but who knew that I had them besides Maddy?

Then it dawned on me that Jax, Jason, and Seth had been sitting in the booth behind me, not to mention the other people in Gil's.

As much as I wanted to believe Jason wasn't my number one suspect, I was still suspicious of him. He'd never explained why he was buying burner phones. With a sigh, I signed into one of my databases and put in Jason's name.

Within seconds I had a lot of information. He was indeed an FBI agent, so he hadn't lied about that, and he had excellent credit. As I went through all available records, I was stunned to learn that up until three years ago, Jason Brock didn't exist. What the hell?

I'd gone as far as I could in this database, so I logged off and ran his name through another database that dug a little deeper and cost me a hefty fee to use every year. The search results showed there were two court records in which his name appeared. Now I was getting somewhere.

The first court record showed a petition for name change from Jason Rockman to Jason Brock! Was he related to the Hope Harbor Rockman's and why would he change his name? What was he trying to hide?

The next court document was the final order approving the name change. Then the trail ended. I sat back in my chair hard.

Figures, just when I start to fall for a guy, he's got major secrets.

I decided to see what I could find out about Jason Rockman. Maybe I could discover why he changed his name.

An hour later I had his original birth certificate, social security number, and where he went to school. He'd attended Quantico.

Now that I had his birth certificate, I may be able to tie him to the Hope Harbor Rockman's. I clicked over to the online genealogy site I use. It didn't take too long to discover he was the great-great-grandson of George Rockman! So, before George's first wife divorced him, they had a child named Elias. Elias married a woman named Evaline, and they had six children, one of them being Henry who was Jason's father. Bingo! Hmm, the name Henry Rockman seemed familiar, but I didn't know why.

I got up and began to pace around the library letting all the new information sink in. Jason's DNA could verify the identity of the skeleton found in the Rockman house. But I still didn't understand why he changed his name. More research was needed.

The newspaper archive site I used gave me the answer - Henry Rockman was in prison for raping and killing two women. Perhaps the apple didn't fall too far from the tree. Oh my God, Jason was the one that arrested him! I couldn't imagine having to arrest your own father for such heinous crimes.

I sat back in my chair, tears welling up in my eyes. Poor Jason. No wonder he changed his name. It all made sense now. I sent the information I'd found to the printer the library had set up for the patrons. I walked over and grabbed the pages as they came out.

I gathered up all the research I'd done on Jason. I'd run it through my shredder when I got home. No one needed to know about Jason's tragic past.

By the time I got back home, the workmen were just packing up to leave. I walked down the hallway to Felix's old room and saw that while it was ready for me to move into, I'd wait until the house was finished.

Karma protested loudly about being locked up in the office all day and did her normal cat zooms around the house before settling down on her cat tree.

Once she was settled, I left to get some dinner.

As I got out of my car in the driveway an hour later, Jason trotted across the street. After we greeted each other, he followed me into the house.

"Wine?" I said, holding up a bottle of white.

He nodded and took the bottle out of my hand. While he opened it, I pulled out a couple of disposable plastic cups.

"Sorry," I said, setting them on the table. "All my wine glasses are packed."

He poured the wine and when he went to sit down at the table, he pushed my bag out of the way. When he did, a couple of the papers I was going to shred slipped out the top and onto the table.

I went to grab them, but he beat me to it. His eyes got wide when he saw what

they were. "You had no right!"

"I was going to shred them. I'm sorry," I said, not able to look at him.

He pulled the rest of the papers out of my bag and skimmed through them. I sat in silence. I knew I should feel ashamed for what I'd done, but I didn't. If he was a serial killer, and responsible for all deaths, I needed to stop him.

"Satisfied now?" he said and turned to face me. His face was red, the veins on his neck were sticking out, and his eyes were cold and hard.

"I really am sorry, Jason," I said, my eyes filling with tears. "It's just that…" and I stopped. There was no way I was going to be able to justify my actions to him, even though I knew my reasons were valid.

Jason turned away from me and headed down the hallway to my office. I followed him. He flicked on the light and crossed the distance to the shredder in three strides. I leaned against the door jamb and watched him shred the documents that revealed his true identity.

When he'd finished, he brushed past me, almost knocking me down, and walked back toward the kitchen. The slamming of the front door caused me to jump, and I slid down the wall in the hallway and buried my face in my hands. *And this is why you don't have any friends, and why all your relationships fail. You're just too nosy for your own good.*

I picked myself off the floor, locked the door and checked the windows before climbing the stairs to go to bed. Karma followed but kept her distance. Even she was pissed at me.

CHAPTER NINETEEN

When Dustin arrived the next morning, we chatted for a few minutes while I made a pot of coffee, then I settled in at my desk to read my emails.

Henry Daniels had sent me scanned copies of Lacey's phone usage for the last three months. There were over one hundred pages. Teenagers! I shook my head and dug in.

Running all the telephone numbers she called would have to wait. Right now, I was more interested in the texts. It took a little searching through the massive amounts of documents, but I finally found the beginning of her talking to Robert away from the chat room. I went through and printed out the texts between him and Lacey so I could highlight the parts I wanted.

As I read through the texts between Robert and Lacey, it became clear that he was working hard to gain her trust. He gave her lots of compliments and said all the things an insecure teenage girl wants to hear. Whoever Robert was, he was smooth.

I also noticed that, when Lacey said something he didn't like, he was quick to reprimand her, and she would beg for forgiveness. As I read through their exchanges, I was feeling sick to my stomach. He played her so easily, and he even got her to send him rather sexy pictures of herself, but always made her pose in what I thought were demeaning and submissive poses.

When she would send the pictures he asked for, he would praise her, and if she did something wrong he would quit talking to her for a while, leaving her devastated and promising to do better.

I had to stop. My whole body was shaking in anger, and my fingers were trembling so bad I couldn't hold the pages steady enough to read. I put the papers on the side table and closed my eyes.

Jason's words about a security system echoed in the back of my mind. Maybe I did need one.

Two hours of research later, I'd found the system I wanted and called the company to have it installed. I added a few more cameras than I probably needed, but better safe than sorry as recent events had taught me. I delayed installation until after the renovations were complete. I just couldn't handle any more workmen in my house right now.

I needed a break, so I got Karma settled in my office and headed into town for an early lunch, since I'd skipped breakfast. Saturdays are rather busy in Hope Harbor as many people are out running errands, stopping for a bite to eat, or just enjoying a beautiful fall day by taking a stroll through town or on the boardwalk by the lake.

Gil's wasn't as busy as I thought it would be; I must have hit at the right time. I found a booth in the back and ordered a bacon omelet and a coffee. Then I sat back in the booth to take a couple of minutes to relax.

I saw Willow, the teenager I'd met in the park, walk by the front window. She stopped and peeked inside. The waitress delivered my food, and when she left, Willow was standing by my table.

"Hi," she said in a voice barely above a whisper. "Can I talk to you?"

"Sure, sit down," I said. "Are you hungry?"

Of course, she's hungry, she's a teenager.

"A little." She pulled a small change purse out of her pocket and began to count her money.

"Order what you want. It's on me," I said.

Willow smiled and, when the waitress appeared, she ordered a pop, hamburger, and fries. I hid a smile as I remembered how my metabolism used to let me eat like that.

"What's up?" I said, cutting into my omelet.

"I'm so scared," she said. She looked at me with her clear blue eyes. "That Robert guy Lacey was talking to. He private messaged me on chat last night."

I dropped my fork on my plate. Damn it! I'd been so busy I hadn't had time for the chat room. I'd wanted him to come after me. "He what? What did he say?"

"Well," she said. She took a long drink of the soda the waitress had delivered. "He just said, 'hello gorgeous.'"

"Did you answer him?"

"No, I was so upset I left chat. I don't know what to do?" she said. Her eyes were scanning the restaurant.

I leaned toward her. "Stay out of chat. You didn't give him your phone number, did you?"

She shook her head. "No. I told you I didn't say a word to him."

"Just making sure. Did you tell your parents?"

"Oh, please," she said, rolling her eyes. "When they're not at work, they are either drunk or fighting. They don't even know I'm there most of the time."

My heart went out to her. I knew how hard it was to live with an alcoholic parent and always feel you're in the way.

"I'm sorry, Willow," I said. "I know how that feels."

She looked at me. I told her a little about my life after my father had committed suicide, and how I'd grown up with an alcoholic mother. Willow listened intently, her eyes filling with tears.

"How did you deal with it?" she said, using her napkin to dab at her eyes.

"I knew if I wanted out, I had to be able to support myself. So that's what I did. I studied hard and worked harder. Plus, I had my Uncle Felix. I don't know if I would have survived without him," I said.

We spent a few minutes talking about Felix and me telling her how he helped me.

"I don't have anyone like that," she said and sighed.

"You have me," I said. I felt a strange kinship with her and wanted to help her. After all Felix had done for me, I had a need to pay it forward.

"Thanks," she said. I saw her visibly relax.

We spent the next hour talking about her grades, and what she wanted to do after high school.

I gave her my cell number before paying the bill and we both left the restaurant. I watched her walk down the sidewalk in the opposite direction. She looked like a scared mouse, all hunched over and scurrying along the sidewalk. I remembered when I felt that way, and my heart broke for her.

As I walked home, I thought about my conversation with Willow and the recent murders. The killings seemed to be escalating. There were three murders in two years, and now there were two in just as many months. It also dawned on me that I hadn't heard from my stalker for a while. What had happened to change the patterns?

It was obvious from my talk with Willow that the predator was already stalking his next victim. Something had forced him to change his mind, his pattern, and I was determined to figure out what it was.

When I got home, the workmen were just leaving, and Jason was waiting for me on the front porch.

"Kitchen's done except for the backsplash. You can move your stuff into the cabinets," Dustin said, smiling from ear to ear.

I thanked him. Jason and I exchanged greetings before going into the house to look at the kitchen. The white cabinets and quartz countertops looked amazing. We spent a few minutes exploring and checking everything out.

"Want me to get the kitchen boxes out of the garage for you?" he asked.

"That would be great, thanks."

Jason carried in all the boxes, and while I was putting everything away, he said he'd be right back and hurried off. He returned carrying a bottle of wine. "You need to celebrate."

We dug through the rest of the boxes to find the corkscrew and two wine glasses and toasted the new kitchen.

I told Jason what I'd been thinking about on the way back from town.

He set his wine glass down on the kitchen table. "Maybe it's not the killer that changed his pattern, maybe it's you."

"What do you mean?" I sat down to join him.

"Think about it. You've changed a lot since you've moved here. You learned how to use a gun, you've shown this guy that no matter what he does, you're not backing off. This killer likes insecure young women. You have become confident and strong."

I leaned back in my chair and thought about what he'd said. It was true.

"Did anyone ever find where Ashley was murdered?" I said, as I collapsed a box so it would lie flat.

"Yes, there's an old abandoned gas station off of Thirty-Two Mile Road. The state police found it a few days after Ashley's body was found. It was set up pretty much the same way Lacey's was. Same book, same type of table with shackles." He shook his head. "We found some evidence, but the lab wasn't sure there was enough DNA to extract a sample. We're waiting to hear."

"So, the FBI has taken over the case?" I said. I refilled our wine glasses.

"We're working in tandem with Seth and the state police."

He got up and tied a stack of empty flat boxes together with twine. Do you want me to put these into the garage?"

I nodded, thinking about what he'd just told me. I knew the DNA was a long shot; if there wasn't a match in the system, the whole case could come to a standstill.

Jason left a little while later, and I retrieved the case files on the other girls' murders from the attic. After pouring myself another glass of wine, I settled into my office to review their files.

By around midnight I'd finished going through all the files and filled in a lot of information on my board. After changing into my pajamas and getting another glass of wine, I settled into my desk chair and studied the board.

It was abundantly clear the same person committed all the murders, right down to the book he'd left at each of the primary crime scenes. Each young woman had been buried face down with their eyes glued shut, and the injuries they'd suffered were pretty much the same. Yet they were murdered hundreds of miles away from each other.

So, what made him hang around Hope Harbor and commit two murders so close together? The other victims were murdered six months to a year apart. The only variable was the murder of Uncle Felix. My gut was telling me Felix got too close in figuring out who this guy is, and that's why he was murdered. There had to be something I was missing.

By 2 a.m. my eyes were burning, and my head was pounding. I had to get some sleep. After double checking all the doors and windows, I went to go upstairs to bed but remembered I hadn't seen Karma since I'd gotten home from dinner. Where the hell was she?

I stood in the middle of the empty living room. "Karma," I said, looking around to see which direction she would come from. But she didn't appear. I searched every inch of the house, but to no avail. This was the last thing I needed at this hour of the night.

"Karma!" I was panicked. Did she get out of the house somehow? Then I heard a faint meow coming from the direction of the kitchen. I'd already searched the kitchen.

I walked in the direction of her plaintive mewing and realized it was coming from the basement. The door was open. I never leave the basement door open. What the hell?

I felt a trickle of sweat run down my spine, my palms were moist, and a ball of fear twisted around in my stomach. I ran into my office and with trembling fingers unlocked the file cabinet to retrieve Felix's gun. I made sure it was loaded before turning on the basement light and cautiously creeping down the stairs.

Karma's mewing was becoming frantic, and I knew she was in trouble. Throwing caution to the wind, I bolted down the remaining stairs, stopping at the bottom to look around. I didn't see anyone, but there were a few places someone could hide. Karma's cries were coming from the rear of the basement by a stack of boxes.

Slowly I worked my way in the opposite direction, searching every nook and cranny. Just when I thought I was alone, one of the boxes that'd been stacked in the back corner moved and I heard Karma cry out.

I ran over to the box. It was duct taped shut, but I could hear Karma crying inside it. What the hell? I grabbed the end of the tape and ripped it off, opening the box to find Karma inside. Her feet had been duct taped together!

"Oh my God!" I grabbed her out of the box and worked as fast as I could to set her free. I ended up having to take her upstairs and cut the tape binding her legs together. I held her close and sobbed.

When I was satisfied, she was okay, I gave her some extra food and darted back into the basement. There, in the box where she'd been held captive, was a note on a dead mouse. It said, "curiosity killed the cat."

"But satisfaction brought it back, you son of a bitch!" I screamed. The basement absorbed the sound like a blanket.

CHAPTER TWENTY

I carried the note and dead mouse upstairs, wrapped the poor dead creature in a paper towel, and took him outside to the garbage. I had to figure out how the creep who did that to Karma got into the house and make sure they couldn't do it again.

After retrieving a flashlight from the kitchen, I started to walk around the perimeter of the house, Felix's gun in hand. Because of the age of the house, the basement windows are larger than the more modern ones, and there are two windows on each side of the house and two in the back.

The two in the back were secure. I walked to the left side of the house and tried the windows there. The first one I tried opened easily. The flashlight revealed fresh scrape marks where someone had used a screwdriver or other tool to pry the window open. Damn it!

I stomped back into the house and locked the basement door. That would have to do for the night, it was nearly 3 a.m. and Dustin and his crew would be here in a few hours.

Wearily, I climbed the stairs to bed with Karma in my arms and Felix's gun tucked into the waistband of my jeans. I was so upset about the events of the evening that I tossed and turned most of the night before falling into a fitful sleep filled with images of dead cats and mice. Every little noise sent me scrambling out of bed and grabbing Felix's gun, only to discover that no one was in the house.

When Dustin got there the next morning, I asked him how to secure the basement windows, and he suggested replacing them with glass block. While he didn't do that type of work, one of his buddies, Marcus, did, and he gave me his number.

Without hesitation I dialed the number and arranged for Marcus to replace the windows that day. Awesome.

I poured myself a strong cup of coffee and fussed around in my office most of the morning trying to fill some work orders. Dustin popped his head in to tell me that Marcus was getting started on the windows and that made me feel a little more secure.

Karma, who'd stayed close by me since I rescued her last night, seemed no worse for wear and napped in her bed on my desk. Everything appeared normal, but in my heart, I knew things were escalating quickly and I had to figure out who was behind the murders and fast. With Jason off my suspect list, the only one left was the mysterious Robert; the game of cat and mouse would start tonight.

With my mind made up, I spent the rest of the day making my clients happy by getting their much-needed research completed. During the day, Bea called and asked me over for dinner, which I happily accepted.

By the time I was done, Dustin and his crew were just finishing up for the day, and Marcus and his crew were on the last basement window. I gave Marcus a check before heading next door to Bea's house.

After we exchanged greetings, Bea led me into the living room for a cocktail, and I settled into one of her brocade-covered winged back chairs. She brought me a glass of wine and sat down on the couch.

I told her what had happened to Karma the night before, and how I'd fixed the problem with the new windows. Bea listened intently, her eyes growing wide as I talked.

"Lord have mercy!" she said. "Who would do such a thing?"

Atlas had settled down next to me, and I stroked his massive head absently. "I don't know," I said. I didn't want to scare her.

Bea picked an invisible piece of lint off one of the throw pillows. "Did you call the police?"

"No." I set my wine glass down on the coaster she had placed on the end table. "I didn't see the point."

She leaned toward me. "Zoey, everyone in town knows you think Felix was murdered and Henry Daniels asked you to find out who killed Lacey. Please, don't lie just to spare my feelings."

I hung my head in shame. I felt horrible. Of course, she knew. There's no such thing as a secret in Hope Harbor. "I'm sorry, Bea," was all I could manage to squeak out.

She reached out and patted my hand. "It's okay. Now, tell me who your suspects are."

Over a fabulous pot roast dinner, I told her almost everything I knew. I started at the beginning and finished up with the events of last night. The words tumbled from my mouth like dice. It was nice to have someone to talk to about all this. I held a few tidbits of information back, but that was more for her safety. I'd never do anything to put her in danger.

Bea listened with fascination, nodding occasionally; I could tell she was hanging on every word.

When I finished, she sat back in her chair and closed her eyes. "Give me a minute."

While she was processing all the information, I got up and cleared the table. I started the kettle for tea and rinsed the dishes before putting them in the dishwasher.

"So, what's your plan with this guy in the chat room?" she asked. She got up and got two mugs for the tea out of a cupboard.

"I'm not sure," I said and shrugged. "I guess I want to get his attention, arrange to meet him somewhere, and then have the police there waiting for him."

Bea nodded. "But, in the meantime, how are you going to keep yourself safe?"

I poured our tea and sat back down at the table. Bea joined me. "I'm having an alarm system installed. I planned on waiting until all the renovations are finished, but I think I'm going to move up the installation date."

"Yes." She set her mug down on the table and smoothed the tablecloth with her hand. "That seems prudent, but I insist you take Atlas in the meantime."

"Oh, Bea, I couldn't!" I said, looking at the large dog that'd been glued to my side the entire night. "You need him with you."

"Oh, hush." She waved her hand. "I have an ulterior motive. I want to go to the casino in Mt. Pleasant with the Mavens of Mayhem for a few days, but I don't have anyone to watch him, and I can't bear to send him to one of those boarding places. You'd actually be doing me a favor."

"The Mavens of Mayhem?" I said and raised an eyebrow. This was a side to Bea I'd never seen before.

"My mahjong group – we meet once a week to play mahjong, and gossip," she said and smiled. "Once in a while we all take a short trip together. This time we decided on the casino."

I got up from my chair. "I see. Well, then I'd be happy to take Atlas for you."

Ten minutes later Bea helped me carry a large bag of dog food, canned dog food, treats, and Atlas' leash across the lawn to my house. Atlas raced ahead of us, his tail wagging. I had to admire his enthusiasm.

Once I got him settled and made sure Karma and Atlas were going to cohabit well, I went into my office with a glass of wine and fired up my computer. I used my photo editing software to take a composition of different pictures of blonde, pretty girls, and combine them into one passable profile picture that matched Robert's type.

Then I signed into the chatroom, added the new picture, and tried to catch up on the conversation before jumping in with both feet. The other teenagers were talking about trouble they were having at school and with their parents. Well, my story had them beat.

I started telling them about my childhood – my father committing suicide, and my mother being an alcoholic. At least I didn't have to lie. It didn't take long for the kids to be empathetic to my situation. Moreover, it took less than twenty-five minutes for me to be private messaged by Robert. Perfect!

He started out smooth and sympathetic to my situation. He would say things like, "I'm so sorry you have to go through this," "Just know I'm here for you if you need to talk," etc. All the things I needed to hear fifteen years ago. Now it was just pissing me off.

We continued to private message each other for about an hour and I just couldn't take it anymore. I felt nauseous, and I was so angry my hands were trembling, making it difficult to type. Saying I had to study for a test, I attempted to leave the chatroom, but not before Robert made me promise I'd be in the chatroom tomorrow. Disgusting.

I let Atlas out into the backyard, rinsed out my wine glass, and gave Karma a few treats for being so well-behaved with our new house guest. A few minutes later, the dog came bounding back to the door, and I let him in, double checking to make sure I deadbolted the door. After checking all the other doors and windows, I headed up to bed.

I'd never realized how small my queen bed was until I had to share it with a hundred plus pound dog and a cat, but I had to admit I felt safer with Atlas' hulking body lying next to me. Maybe I did need a boyfriend.

I woke up the next morning to Atlas' frantic barking. I tumbled out of bed and scampered down the stairs. Atlas was standing at the front door, his ears back, and his hair standing on end. Over the noise of the vicious barking, I heard someone calling my name.

I grabbed Atlas by the collar and opened the door. Seth was standing there with two coffees and an interesting-looking box from the bakery. I stepped aside to let him enter, and Atlas gave him the once over before trotting to the back door.

"What the hell did you do?" Seth said, striding into the kitchen.

I wiped the sleep from my eyes. "Huh? Let me get my head together."

I let the dog out and fed Karma. Following Bea's instructions, I dumped exactly a cup and a half of dog food into Atlas' bowl and a can of dog food. I let the dog in and turned my attention back to Seth.

He was standing at the kitchen counter dishing out two cinnamon rolls. "The Mavens of Mayhem!"

"Bea's group? What are you talking about?" I asked and retrieved two forks from one of the drawers.

Seth pulled out a chair and sat down. He met my eyes with a venomous glare. "I was greeted at the police station this morning by a group of older women calling themselves the Mavens of Mayhem. They demanded that I prove to them and to you that I was working on Felix's and Lacey's murders. And why didn't you report the break-in the night before last?"

As he talked, I started to chuckle, the visual image was just too much. "Sorry. I had no idea," I said, doubling over with laughter.

He slammed his fist down on the table. "It's not funny!"

That made me laugh even harder, and he waited patiently while I collected myself.

"Sorry," I said, wiping my teary eyes with a napkin.

"Now, tell me what happened the other night," he said.

I told him what happened to Karma and how the person got into the house. Recounting the events made me angry all over again. "What was the point in calling the police? The damage was already done, and I've taken steps to make sure it never happens again."

He nodded towards Atlas. "The dog?"

"That's part of it. He belongs to one of the Mavens of Mayhem," I said and chuckled as the image of a mob of angry women facing off against Seth popped back into my mind. "I'm also having an alarm system installed this week."

He winced when I mentioned the Mavens but didn't comment.

Atlas walked over to him, and he patted the dog's head. "He seems like a good dog. He managed to find Ashley's body." He shook his head. "Scared me when he barked this morning."

I looked at Atlas. His tongue was hanging out the side of his mouth, and he was looking up at Seth with adoring eyes. "He flunked out of the police academy."

Seth chuckled. "The Mavens mentioned something about a chatroom? And that's how you think the killer is meeting his victims?"

"Yes," I said.

"How did you find out about that?"

"I was talking to some teenagers that hang out at the park, and they told me about it. Plus, Lacey was talking to some guy calling himself Robert. But I'm sure you already know that." I rose from the table and picked up our plates.

He nodded. "Stay out of the chatroom, Zoey."

Before I could respond, Atlas ran to the front door and started to bark. I glanced at the clock – 9 a.m. Dustin was here, and I was still in my pajamas.

I sighed and went to answer the door.

Dustin endured a rather rowdy greeting from Atlas, and Karma headed for higher ground in my office.

"I have to run," Seth said, as he opened the front door.

We said our good-byes, and I raced up the stairs to throw on my running clothes.

When I returned, Dustin told me they would be finished with the bedroom and living room that day, and I could have the furniture delivered. Finally!

After calling the furniture store, I put Atlas on his leash and took him running with me. Sadly, he burned out long before I did, and after only a mile I had to turn around and walk him back toward the house. It was obvious we were going to have to work on his endurance so he could go the whole five miles with me.

I gave him a bowl of water, and after my shower, went into my office to get some work done. There was an email from Henry Daniels with a copy of Lacey's autopsy report attached. I sighed. I felt terrible for asking him to get it, but there just wasn't another way. I wrote him back and gave him an update on what I'd found out and promised to keep him updated more often.

Eagerly, I opened the autopsy report and settled in for an afternoon of reading.

CHAPTER TWENTY-ONE

The autopsy report read pretty much as expected: buried face down, eyes glued shut, naked. Her injuries were in line with the assaults the other girls had suffered before they were killed. I updated my murder board with new information.

As I walked into the kitchen to pour another cup of coffee, it hit me. What happened to Lacey's clothes? And Ashley's? I dashed back to my office and called Jax.

After we exchanged greetings, I asked him about the clothes.

"Clothes? No," he said, rather hesitantly. "We didn't find any clothes at either crime scene. I know we searched the area between the grave and the Rockman house."

I took notes on what he told me. "So, do you and Seth think the killer kept them as souvenirs?" I knew the clothes weren't in the Rockman house, or they would have been found.

"It's possible I suppose." I heard a whirring noise in the background as he talked.

"I'll catch up with Seth this morning and see if he's located them. I need to go. I have to finish shaving and get to the gym."

Electric razor. That was the sound I heard. We hung up, and I sat in my chair for quite a while trying to piece things together in my head.

Atlas came bounding into my office and started to whine. I got up and released him into the backyard. I stepped outside and saw him running around, nose to the ground, tracking something. That gave me an idea.

I called Henry and asked him if he had any of Lacey's clothes left, and if I could borrow one of her shirts. He said they did, and I arranged to pick it up at his office in a half-hour.

I locked Karma in my office with her food and a clean bowl of water, then grabbed a large plastic storage bag and tucked it in my purse before putting Atlas into my Jeep and heading into town.

Henry met me at the door to his house and I took the shirt he gave me and put it in the plastic storage bag I'd brought along with me. I wanted to preserve as much of the scent as I could. Even though Atlas flunked out of doggy police training, it didn't mean he wasn't a good tracking dog. After all, only the elite dogs made it through the rigorous training.

Fifteen minutes later, we were headed out to Lacey's burial site. Atlas loved the car ride and kept his head hanging out the window and barking at almost anything that moved. I couldn't help but laugh, and he helped brighten my mood. Did I need a dog?

I pulled all the way down the driveway and parked behind the Rockman house. I let Atlas out to run around for a few minutes while I retrieved Lacey's shirt and my messenger bag that I put crossways around my body.

After putting Atlas on his leash, I pulled the shirt out of the plastic bag and held it up to the dog's nose, letting him get a good whiff of Lacey's scent. He immediately put his nose to the ground and started pulling me across the yard. What the hell?

Even though I was in good shape, I was still having a hard time keeping up with the rambunctious dog. I tripped on the uneven ground, and the leash came out of my hand as I fell to the ground. Damn it!

I scrambled to my feet and saw Atlas pawing frantically at the closed barn door, his frantic barking and whining caused me to pick up my pace. When I opened the barn door, he ran inside. I'd assumed the police had searched the barn when Lacey's primary crime scene was found, but I couldn't be sure.

Pausing only long enough to pull my flashlight out of my bag, I walked into the barn to find Atlas. It took a minute for my eyes to adjust to the semi-darkness of the cavernous structure. Light filtered in through the gaps in the walls, and I shone my flashlight around trying to find the dog.

I could hear him whining, and the sound of something thrashing around coming from one of the horse stalls toward the back of the musty barn.

When I arrived at the stall, Atlas was whining and launching himself at an old ladder that led to the loft. As he jumped, rotten hay was being thrown everywhere, and the smell made me gag.

"Good boy," I said, kneeling down and calling him over to me.

Atlas wagged his tail and sat down, his brown eyes glinted with excitement, his whole body was trembling. I kissed his nose and tousled his ears. "You like the thrill of the hunt as much as I do, don't ya, boy?" He licked my face in response. Yuck.

"Stay here." I held the flashlight in my mouth, and started to go up the rickety ladder, testing each step before giving it my full weight.

I got to the top and played the flashlight across the loft. I could see bales of decomposing hay laying haphazardly, an old trunk, a couple of antique milk cans, and an old pitchfork.

The floorboards of the loft didn't appear to be in good condition, so I got on my knees and inched my way towards the back of the loft, hanging onto beams whenever possible. I paused when I saw the thin layer of hay disturbed in one area, like someone had crawled or scooted across the floor, just like I was doing.

The trail led to the old trunk. Now what? If I used my bare hands and opened the trunk, I would be destroying any fingerprints or other evidence. I looked around the loft for something I could use. Not finding anything, I grabbed a bunch of hay in each hand. Gross. I used the hay to open the trunk. It was empty. What the hell?

I heard Atlas whine and bark from the stall below me. He must have been tracking my progress from the first floor of the barn. "Hang on, boy. Almost finished."

I sat up on my knees and let the flashlight explore the immediate area I was in. Something white caught the light by two hay bales that were side by side. I inched forward and saw it was a white garbage bag filled with something.

It took a couple of minutes for me to retrieve the old pitchfork a few feet away from me, and I used it to snag the garbage bag and pull it out of its hiding place. I illuminated the bag with my flashlight and saw some bunched-up women's clothes with blood on them. From what I could see, some of them resem-bled the clothes Lacey and Ashley were wearing when they dis-appeared. Bingo!

Leaving the bag there, I made my way back to the ladder as fast as I could. I climbed down, praised Atlas for a job well done, and called 9-1-1.

I took Atlas out of the barn, and we sat down on the ground waiting for the police to arrive. A few minutes later, Seth and

Jason pulled down the driveway at the same time, and a crime scene investigation unit pulled in behind them.

"The loft," I said and pointed to the barn. Seth nodded and pulled his pickup over by the barn with the CSI in tow. Jason pulled in next to my Jeep and parked.

"How did you find them?" He plucked a few pieces of hay out of my hair.

"Atlas found them really. What are you doing here?" I said.

"I was in Seth's office when you called and decided to tag along." He looked down at the dog. "How did he find them?"

I told him about the day's events.

He knelt down and petted the dog. "Good boy!" Atlas wagged his tail in reply.

"Why don't you get out of here. We'll talk later," he said, his eyes on the barn.

I nodded, put Atlas into my Jeep and slowly drove down the driveway to the main road.

When I got home, I released Karma from my office and got Atlas a bowl of ice-cold water and a few treats before heading upstairs to take a shower. I felt as if the putrid smell of the barn had permeated every pore of my body and I couldn't wait to scrub myself clean.

By the time I got dressed and back downstairs, Dustin was finishing up and told me they'd be finished with the bathroom by the end of the week. Awesome!

I microwaved a bowl of soup and headed into my office to catch up. After going through my emails, it was painfully clear that tomorrow was going to be a workday. I signed into the chatroom and started chatting with some of the teenagers.

Two hours later, Robert still hadn't messaged me, and I didn't see his user-name in the chatroom. Maybe the killer was taking a day off – or had another victim.

A feeling of panic welled up in my stomach. I raced to the kitchen, pulled my phone out of my bag, and dialed Willow's number. She answered on the second ring.

After making sure she was at home and safe, I could breathe a sigh of relief. I took Atlas outside and checked to make sure the house was locked up before climbing wearily into bed.

Atlas woke me up the next morning by standing over me and licking my face. Ugh! He must need to go outside. I let him out and started my coffee. It was seven-thirty. I'd overslept.

I changed into my running clothes and grabbed Atlas before trotting out the door. The dog did a better job of keeping up with me today, and we managed a strong three miles instead of walking most of the way back.

The furniture showed up before Dustin arrived and it didn't take long for them to unload and put all the furniture in place before the workmen got started for the day.

I spent a few minutes making my new bed. I'd move my clothes and other stuff downstairs once they were finished with the bathroom. I poured a cup of coffee and was just heading into my office to fill some work orders, when Jason poked his head around the front door. I waved him into my office, and after getting a cup of coffee, he closed my office door and sat down in the chintz chair.

"It's been confirmed. The clothes you found belonged to Ashley and Lacey," he said.

"That's what I thought," I said. "Thanks."

Jason got up and walked over to the large murder board. "It makes sense but doesn't make sense at the same time." He shook his head.

I got up and stood beside him. "I know. I wish Felix were here; he'd be able to figure it out."

Jason nodded. "Do you still have the files of the other girls?"

"Yes, I'll be right back," I said and walked out of my office. On the way to my bedroom I grabbed the stepstool and a flashlight out of the kitchen.

I went into my bedroom and shut the door. It only took a couple of minutes for me to scamper up into the attic to retrieve the lockbox. I put away the stool and flashlight and returned to my office.

"They're in here. Help yourself, but you can't take them out of this room."

He took the files out of the lockbox and settled back into the chintz chair. I dashed into the living room and grabbed a couple of folding trays out of the front closet. I sat them up for him so he could put his coffee down and read the files at the same time. Then I sat down at my desk to get some work done.

Atlas found his way into my office and lay down at Jason's feet. Karma made herself comfortable on the cat post in front of the window.

We worked in companionable silence for most of the morning until Jason got a telephone call and had to leave. After he'd gone, the room felt empty and a profound sense of loneliness washed over me.

Shaking it off, I walked over to the tray tables to see what he'd been looking at. I sank into the chair. It was still warm from Jason's body, and I snuggled into the lingering scent of his cologne.

He'd been comparing the police reports from the first two murders. I'd already done that. Had I missed something? It was late afternoon before I stopped. Nothing in the files jumped out at me, and I had work to do.

By 2 a.m. I'd gotten caught up with my clients and went to bed.

I left Atlas at home the next morning while I went for my run. I wanted to think about the case, and he was a distraction. As I trotted around the cemetery, I remembered Jason telling me that Ashley's primary crime scene was an abandoned gas station out on Thirty-Six Mile road. I'm sure the police had found everything so there wasn't any point going out there. But it made me wonder about other abandoned houses and buildings in the area. Definitely worth checking out.

After my shower, I called Jason and asked him if he still had the list of abandoned buildings in the area the FBI had come up with.

"I know where you're going with this, Zoey," he said. "I'd prefer you didn't, but I know there's no stopping you." I heard the sound of fingers on a keyboard through the phone. "Check your email. Take Atlas and stay in touch."

"Thanks!" I said, but he'd already hung up.

CHAPTER TWENTY – TWO

I printed out the list and plugged the four locations into the GPS on my cell phone. Before leaving I made sure I had everything I could possibly need - water for both Atlas and me, a pry bar, flashlight, latex gloves, my digital camera, cell phone, and Felix's gun.

Atlas willingly jumped into the Jeep; he was so excited he was trembling. I knew he loved our adventures, and he'd probably not experienced this much activity since Bea's husband died.

We headed north out of Hope Harbor and ended up at an old, small farmhouse. I let Atlas off his leash and since the front door was open, let him run around the house. I could hear his nails clicking on the floors, but he didn't seem to be too excited about anything. I followed and checked the first floor. The stairs leading to the second floor were pretty rotted out, and I knew there was no point in even trying to explore up there. If I couldn't make it up the stairs, there's no way the killer could.

I called to Atlas, and he came scampering out of the house. We soon knocked off the second location, an old barn and foundation of a house that once stood on the property, and then set our sights on location number three.

According to Jason's list, it was an abandoned church – the only building still standing after one of the mining towns that used to be in the area shut down. It took a while to find because Mother Nature had reclaimed the land.

I pulled down what used to be a road that led to the property. We could only go so far because of the underbrush. I put the dog on his leash, grabbed my messenger bag, and as we started to walk, Atlas, who'd had his nose to the ground, let out a shrill bark and started to pull me down the old road. The grasses and underbrush looked a bit trampled, as if someone had been down there recently. This looked promising.

After making Atlas stop long enough for me to pull the gun out of my bag, we continued down the path. I had to force the dog to slow down, and soon my arm began to ache from the effort.

Within a few minutes, a small, stone structure came into view through the branches of the trees. That had to be the church. Atlas, who was still tracking, seemed to become more agitated as we got closer to the building.

I knew I couldn't hold him and defend myself if I had to, so I let him off his lead and let him bound ahead of me. At least if someone was there, Atlas would flush them out. It was kind of nice to have an early warning system.

By the time I caught up with the dog, he was standing outside the door of the church panting and wagging his tail. I pulled the gun out of the waistband of my jeans and eased the safety off.

"You ready, boy?" I said, my voice barely a whisper.

I put my hand on the door handle and slowly opened the heavy, wooden door. Atlas leaped ahead of me, and I turned on my flashlight before entering the building. No one was there, thank goodness.

There were four rows of pews covered with dust and spider webs that lined either side of the center aisle. An altar stood on an elevated platform at the front of the church and when I got closer, I saw new white candles, a wooden pentagram, and a copy of the book that'd been left at all the murder scenes.

Six lead glass windows, three on each side, let in what little sunlight managed to make its way through the canopy of trees, casting eerie shadows around the church.

The stale air was filled with a musty aroma, and the fresh air streaming in from the open door brought little relief.

Atlas was scratching at a door at the back of the altar platform, so I moved forward to investigate. The church was giving me the creeps, and every hair on my body was standing on end. The atmosphere seemed to affect Atlas as well, because his normal excitement seemed subdued.

I opened the door at the back of the altar. Instead of bounding ahead of me like he normally does, Atlas stayed glued to my side. We crept forward, and were just over the threshold, when the beam from my flashlight landed on a wall of photographs. What the hell?

Before moving forward, I let my flashlight explore the rest of the room. There was an old wooden desk and various tall candle holders that must have once been by the alter. They held six candles each. A small gas generator sat next to the desk along with a red gas can. A surge strip with four outlets sat on the floor next to the generator, and the cords coming out of it led to a light above the picture wall and a desk lamp.

I walked over to look at the various photographs. They were all pictures of Lacey, Ashley, and me! The pictures of Lacey and

Ashley were crossed out in angry-looking red magic marker. "It's a killing board," I whispered. "This has to be his lair." Chills ran up and down my spine, and I felt light-headed.

Atlas must have sensed my anxiety, because he walked over and sat down next to me, nuzzling my hand with his nose. I patted his head and took a couple of deep breaths to calm down – thankful for his presence.

The pictures were of me jogging, at restaurants, in my car, at the grocery store, furniture store, and almost everywhere else I went. There were even a few of me that must have been taken through the windows of my house, and at Dixon's Bookstore. My blood ran cold, and I felt as if I was going to pass out. I plopped down on the cold wooden floor and covered my face with my hands. Tears wanted to come, but I fought them back. I got up and forced myself to continue investigating.

I opened the dark curtains that covered the two windows at the back of the room and let in some light.

After sitting my flashlight down on the desk and fishing my digital camera out of my bag, I took as many pictures as I could, covering every square inch of the small room. When I finished, I put on the pair of latex gloves I'd brought and examined the desk.

An old tin can served as a pencil holder and contained a red magic marker, scissors, and a couple of generic pens.

On top of the desk were three burner phones still in their packages, a tape dispenser, and stapler. I took pictures of all of it.

When I had finished, I pulled out my cell phone and called Jason.

"I found it. There're pictures," I said, breathlessly.

"On the way. I'll call Seth," he said, and hung up.

"But how do you know where I am?" I said to nobody.

I took Atlas outside and opened a bottle of water, letting it trickle out slowly so Atlas could lap it up. We sat down with our backs against a tall oak tree and waited for Jason.

"Zoey?" I heard Jason's voice coming from the path.

"Over here!" I said, standing up to greet him. Before I could grab Atlas, he took off in the direction of Jason's voice.

"Good boy!" I heard him say. "Take me to Zoey."

Within seconds, Jason and Atlas emerged from the woods.

"You okay?" he said, putting his hands on my shoulders.

I stepped away from his grip. "How did you know where I was? I didn't tell you."

"I've been tracking your phone." He bowed his head, not even daring to look at me.

"You what?" I screamed. My hands balled into fists, and I could feel my face flush as anger flooded my body.

He took a step towards me, but Atlas jumped in between us, bared his teeth and growled.

"I was just trying to protect you," he said, stopping in his tracks.

I held up my hand. "Don't even." I called Atlas and snapped on his leash before stomping out of the woods without another word, muttering to myself all the way back to my Jeep. I heard Jason call after me but ignored him.

As I pulled out, I saw Seth and Jax pull in along with a crime scene unit. I pulled off the road into a cemetery and parked my truck. I was trembling so fiercely that I didn't trust myself to drive.

Fear settled into my body and twisted my stomach into knots. I felt violated, not only by the killer, but by Jason as well. Calm down, Zoe, the alarm company is coming tomorrow. You have Atlas, you'll be fine.

I managed to compose myself enough to drive home. After turning Atlas loose in the back yard, I ran through the house closing all the blinds and checking every window.

The dog was barking in the yard, and I looked out the back door to see Bea standing at the side gate. Atlas' tail was wagging so hard his whole back end was wiggling, and he almost knocked himself down.

I opened the back door. "Come around to the front, Bea!" Then I let Atlas in, and he ran to the front entrance. I opened the door and Bea came in the house. After sharing greetings, she spent a few minutes fawning over the dog.

We settled in the living room, and I poured us each a glass of wine.

"So, fill me in on what's been happening since I've been gone," she said, taking a sip of her wine.

I set my glass down on the coffee table and filled her in on everything that had happened, including how indispensable Atlas had been to me.

When I had finished, she leaned forward in her chair. "This is serious business, Zoey. This guy wants you dead, and he's not going to stop unless he's caught."

I nodded. "The alarm system is going in tomorrow. I'll be fine." I didn't sound convincing. Atlas had settled in on the couch next to me. I wasn't a fan of having him on my new furniture but didn't have the heart to chase him down.

We chatted a while longer, and she made me tell her every detail about my adventures.

"Do you want to keep Atlas here for a bit longer? It would make me feel better knowing he was at your side." She looked at the dog who'd put his head on my lap.

I looked from her to the dog. It was obvious Atlas felt he needed to stay close to me. "If you don't mind. That would be great."

"Then it's settled," she said and got up from her chair.

I walked her to the door, and Atlas made no attempt to go home with her. "Thanks, Bea."

She gave me a hug. "Call me if you need anything."

I locked the door behind her, poured another glass of wine, and grabbed my digital camera out of my messenger bag. I wanted to review all the pictures I took at the old church. I just knew I'd missed something.

I plugged the camera into my computer. While I waited for the pictures to download, the rumbling in my stomach reminded me that I hadn't eaten since breakfast, so I ordered a pizza.

I reviewed the pictures one by one, examining each one carefully. My pizza arrived, and I took it into my office along with a glass of diet soda. Karma and the dog followed me; Atlas lay down in front of the door, while Karma opted for her comfy bed on my desk. Everything looked calm and peaceful, but I felt jittery and ill at ease, like a freight train was heading right for me and I couldn't see it.

As I ate, I kept thinking about the old stone church. How had he found it? He had to be familiar with the area, because you couldn't see it from the road. It made me wonder how the FBI knew it was there.

I clicked over to the historical society website and browsed through all the pages and different articles they'd posted. Less than five months ago Jason had posted an article about the history of the old church, along with pictures.

It turned out it was an old Jesuit church, erected when some of the first settlers appeared in the area. The goal was to convert the Native Americans. It hadn't gone well, and the Jesuits were ill prepared for the harsh Michigan winters. They ended up abandoning the area in the spring.

I looked through the pictures. There were no signs that anyone had been there for years, so these had to have been taken before Lacey disappeared. Interesting. Everything on the altar in the pic-tures looked exactly the same as I'd found it today. The beginning of the article contained the general location of the building. Hmm.

After finishing dinner, I let Atlas outside and threw away the pizza box before settling back in to go through the rest of the pictures I'd taken.

As I examined the pictures he'd taken of Lacey, Ashley, and myself, it dawned on me – there weren't any pictures of Willow. What the hell?

CHAPTER TWENTY-THREE

Let's see, there were no pictures of Willow. To me that meant one of two things – either the killer lost interest for some reason, or Willow lied. I was inclined to believe the latter. In my mind, once this guy targeted you, he was relentless until you were dead. I made a mental note to touch base with Willow in the morning and went to bed.

Three big burly guys from the alarm company arrived just as I got back from my run with Atlas. I went over everything with them as far as the placement of the cameras, before running upstairs to get my shower.

Once dressed, I packed up Atlas' things and walked him home. I had to admit I would miss him, although I was pretty sure Karma was glad to see him go. Bea assured me I could borrow him anytime I wanted, and that made me feel a little better.

After getting a cup of coffee, I retreated to my office so I wouldn't be in the way of the alarm company, and dialed Willow's number.

"Willow, did you lie about Robert messaging you in the chat room?" I was a bit upset with her and didn't have time for pleasantries.

"No," she said.

"Tell me the truth. It's important."

"Yes," she said and sighed.

I knew it. "Why would you lie about something like that?" I wasn't ready to let her off the hook.

"I thought," she said, and hesitated.

"You thought what?" I said, my voice firm.

"I thought that if I told you he was after me, you'd let me stay with you and I could get out of this house," she said. I could hear the tears in her voice.

"Oh, for God's sake, Willow!" I ran my hand through my hair. Teenage logic.

"I'm sorry," she said, her voice small.

As I opened my mouth to respond, Jason walked into my office. "I have to go. This isn't over. I'll talk to you later."

I hung up the phone, turned my chair to face Jason, and glared at him.

"Zoey, I'm really sorry," he said, holding his hands out in front of him, face up. "I was so scared something would happen to you. I didn't think."

I stood up - my hands balled into fists at my side. "I've never felt so violated in my life! How dare you track my phone!" I walked up to him, inches from his face.

His face clouded over. "How is this any different than you digging into my background?"

"Everything I found out about you is a matter of public record, if you know where to look! Tracking my phone is completely different!"

His eyes filled with anger. "I don't see how! You invaded my privacy, too!"

Our shouting attracted the attention of the workmen putting in my alarm system and they came running down the hall and into my office. "Everything okay here?" They looked at Jason.

"Everything's fine. I was just leaving," Jason said and walked out of the office. I heard the front door slam as he left.

I plopped down in my chair, shaken. I was visibly trembling. "You okay?" one of the guys asked.

"I'm fine. Thanks." I plastered a smile on my face, and they went back to work.

I distracted myself by diving into the work orders that had piled up, stopping only long enough for the workmen to install the glass break alarm on my office window.

It was late afternoon by the time they'd finished with the alarm, and they spent a good half-hour explaining how everything worked and setting up my cell phone app. Excellent.

After they left, I used the cell phone app to check all the camera angles and turn the alarm on and off. I wanted to make sure I understood exactly what to do should there be an emergency.

I was starving, so I changed out of my sweats and into something more presentable before driving the two short blocks to the Blue Bass to grab some dinner.

When I walked into the restaurant, I saw Seth sitting at a table with two older blonde women. He saw me and waved me over.

He stood up when I got to the table and introduced his Aunt Doreen and his mother, Betsy. We exchanged greetings, and his mother asked me to join them.

"Get her chair," Betsy said, nudging Seth's arm with the back of her hand.

He walked around the table and pulled my chair out for me.

I took my seat and gave him a smile. "Thanks."

Dinner was an uncomfortable affair. His mom criticized or corrected almost everything Seth did and said. He took everything in stride, but I could see the pain and embarrassment in his eyes. I felt sorry for him and tried to deflect by engaging her in conversation, but she was like a dog with a bone - relentless.

His Aunt Doreen, who reminded me of a deflated balloon, sat in her chair, shoulders slumped and arms close to her body. She kept her head down, avoiding eye contact with everyone, and ate her food in small quiet bites. To me it appeared that life, or Betsy, had beaten her down to the point the joy of living had been sucked out of her.

As soon as I had finished eating, I made an excuse to leave and drove home, with Betsy's criticisms of Seth still ringing in my ears. I poured myself a glass of wine to calm my frayed nerves from dinner and went into my office to sign into the chat room.

I scanned the list of people in chat but didn't see Robert's name among them. I hung out for a bit, talking to some of the girls, and within a half-hour Robert popped into chat. Ten minutes later, he private messaged me. We chatted for a few minutes about school, and then he asked for my cell phone number, which I refused to give him. Damn it! I hadn't thought about that. When I refused, he became angry and demeaning. I told him he was scaring me, signed out of chat, and shut down my computer.

Karma followed me into the kitchen, and I gave her a few treats to snack on while I rinsed out my wine glass and put it in the dishwasher. After setting the alarm, I went to bed. I missed Atlas' body cuddled up next to mine, and the harsh words between Jason and me replayed through my head. Maybe I should have cut him a break; after all, his intentions were good. I gave up all hopes of sleep at 4:30 a.m. and rolled out of bed.

After my run the next morning, I ran to the store and bought a burner phone, loaded with a ton of minutes. Now when Robert wanted to play, I at least had a phone number to give him.

On the way home from the store, I stopped at the bakery and picked up two coffees and cinnamon rolls. I pulled into my driveway and walked across the street to Jason's house.

He answered the door wearing a pair of sweatpants and no shirt. His hair was tousled, as if he'd just rolled out of bed. "It's 7 a.m. Don't you sleep?"

"Sorry." I held out the bakery box. "I come bearing gifts of sweet goodness."

He chuckled and stood back to let me in. He took the cinnamon roll box, and I followed him through the sparsely furnished living room into the eat-in kitchen.

While he was dishing up the rolls, I stood next to him at the kitchen counter. "I'm really sorry about yesterday. I over-reacted."

He carried our plates to the table. "I'm sorry, too."

We settled down to eat and chatted about the events of the last couple of days. I felt better knowing things between us were back to normal. The conversation soon turned to the killer's lair in the old stone church.

"I'm really scared for you, Zoey," he said.

I put my fork down on the edge of my plate. "I know. What do you think I should do?"

He shrugged. "Go visit your mom for a while, get out of town until Seth can catch this guy. He's real close."

"No." I shook my head. "What do you mean he's close? Who is it?"

"Seth thinks it could be Jax," he said. "And I agree."

"Jax! It can't be." I sat back in my chair, my mind going a thousand miles an hour.

"I know," Jason said. He reached across the table and squeezed my hand. "I found it hard to accept too."

I shook my head. "I don't believe it. Criminals get caught because they are either sloppy, stupid, or both. Jax isn't sloppy or stupid."

Jason got up and put the plates in the sink. "The evidence is pretty compelling."

"What evidence?" I said.

"Among other things, there were some hairs found on the clothes from the barn. The DNA matched Jax's." He turned around from the sink to face me.

I stood up from the table. "I need to think about this. Talk later."

When I got back across the street, I ran into my office to study the murder board.

The more I thought about it, the more it made perfect sense. He had the opportunity, and it explained Uncle Felix's murder. Felix trusted him. It would be nothing for Jax to slip sleeping pills into Felix's drink and then set it up to look like an accident.

As all the pieces began to click into place, I felt a shot of adrenaline run through my body, causing me to shiver. I paced around my office. I always think better when I pace. I knew Seth was taking a lot of heat in the media for not making an arrest, and, logically, Jax being the killer made sense. But my intuition was telling me Seth was way off on this one – I just had to prove it.

After getting another cup of coffee and letting Dustin in to work on the bathroom, I made myself comfortable in my desk chair. It was going to be a long day.

First, I had to find out if Jax was in the other states at the same time the other girls were murdered. Chloe Manning was from Illinois, Jenny Parker from Nebraska, and Lisa Conrad from Ohio.

I ran a detailed background check on Jax, whose real name was Jaxson Cooper and waited for the results to pop up on my screen. Let's see, Jax was born in Montana, but didn't really show up again until he turned sixteen and his driver's license was issued with a Hope Harbor address. Hmmm, his family must have moved here when he was younger.

At twenty-one he graduated from the local police academy and went to work for a large police department in Illinois a year before Chloe was murdered.

I searched through Chloe's file, but there wasn't any mention of him in any of the reports, so he must not have been involved with that case, which would be normal for a rookie cop – he'd be on traffic duty.

He left Illinois and appeared to have dropped off the radar until two years ago when he moved back to Hope Harbor to work at the police department. So where was he for two years?

Using a different data base, I dug deeper. I pulled a detailed credit history, and saw that, according to utility bills and credit card statements, he'd been in Ohio during the time Jenny was killed, but I couldn't find anything that indicated he'd ever lived in Nebraska.

What I found interesting is that, while he lived in Ohio, he had worked as a long- distance truck driver. I had no way of knowing what routes he drove, so I couldn't say for sure he was never in Nebraska. I did wonder why he walked away from being a police officer during that period of his life, but that didn't make him a killer.

I had no answer for the DNA evidence. No matter how hard I tried, I just couldn't wrap my head around Jax being a killer.

My thoughts were interrupted by a phone call from my mom. She was drunk of course and whining about how no one loved her, and she was all alone. I could sympathize. I was in the same situation. Twenty-five minutes later I convinced her to go lay down and we hung up. Sheesh!

I spent the rest of the day working on client requests and billing. By six o'clock I'd had it and wandered into the kitchen to make myself something to eat. As I was making dinner, I heard a knock at my back door. What the hell?

When I peeked out the blinds, I saw Jax dressed in dark jeans and a black t-shirt. I opened the door. "Why didn't you use the front door?"

He walked into the house, and I shut and locked the door behind him.

"Seth is looking for me. He's going to arrest me for the murders," he said. His eyes were wide with fear. "I swear to you, Zoey, I didn't do it."

I put my hand on his arm. "I know."

We walked into the kitchen. "You believe me?"

"Yes. You'd better tell me the whole story while I make dinner."

"My DNA was found on the clothes, and when they searched my house, they found a copy of the book that'd been left at all the crime scenes."

I diced some more vegetables and added them to the wok. "Okay, what were you doing with the book?"

Jax busied himself setting the table. "Reading it. I was hoping there would be something in there that would give me a clue about who this guy is."

Made sense. I'd done the exact same thing without any tangible results. "And?"

"Nothing," he said and sighed. "I really think the crime scene was staged to throw off the investigation. Make it seem like a ritualistic type of murder, when it really wasn't."

I dished up our dinner and sat down at the table. "I think you're right. But Jax, you need to turn yourself in and get a good lawyer."

He hung his head. "I know. Can I just stay here tonight? I'll call an attorney and turn myself in tomorrow."

"You can take my room," I said.

After dinner I ran upstairs to put fresh sheets on my bed while Jax cleaned up the kitchen.

Wonderful! Now I was harboring a fugitive. Just another interesting item to add to my resume.

When I came downstairs, Jax was parked in front of the TV. "Going to go see if you can hook the killer in the chatroom?"

"Yeah, worth a shot." I disappeared into my office. As I flipped on my computer, it struck me – how did Jax know about the chatroom? Jason must have said something.

CHAPTER TWENTY-FOUR

When I woke up the next morning, Jax was gone. I found a sticky note on the coffeemaker that said, 'Going to end this. Stay home!"

For a split second I thought he was going to kill himself, not able to face the shame of being arrested for murder. I quickly dismissed the thought; Jax wasn't the type. It made much more sense that he was going after the killer. But who was it and where did he go? Damn it, Jax! A little more information wouldn't have killed you.

I poured my coffee and went into my office to boot up my computer. I opened the program I used to trace cell phones and punched in Jax's number. It showed he was at the Rockman house. I thought about calling Seth, but he would only have arrested him. No, if Jax thought he knew who the killer was, maybe I could help him.

It only took a few minutes for me to get dressed and pack up my flashlight and pry bar in case I had to take the wood off the window again. When I opened the front door to leave, Seth was standing there.

"And where are you going with a pry bar in your hand?" he said raising an eyebrow.

"I...ahh ..." I could feel my face turning red. "Jax was here last night, but he's gone now. He thinks he knows who the killer is."

Seth's face clouded over, and he set his jaw. "I think you better make us some coffee and tell me everything. I hate being kept in the dark."

I sighed and tucked the pry bar into my bag before setting it down on the couch. I turned around and walked into the kitchen to make coffee. It was going to be a long morning.

When he followed me into the kitchen, I caught a whiff of his cologne, and the scent caused something in my brain to stir. But what was it?

I busied myself pouring the coffee, and turned around to face him, a cup of coffee in each hand.

Seth turned around to face me. "What? Why are you looking at me that way?"

"Am I? Stand still a second." I sat the cups down on the kitchen island and moved behind him and pretended to brush something off his shoulders. "Much better," I said as I breathed in his cologne.

A few weeks ago, I would have found the scent of him exciting. Not this time. That's what the alarm bells had triggered when he walked in. I knew this cologne.

The man who attacked me in the house had worn it. So, it was Seth! My mind began to spin, and adrenaline scorched my veins as it raced through my body. I was finding it hard to breathe. Calm down, Zoe. Keep your wits about you. I forced myself to take a couple of deep breaths.

My eyes met his, and he knew I'd figured it out.

"Why, Seth?" I said, edging myself closer to the door.

"You met my mother. You have to ask?"

"What does your mother have to do with you killing five women?" I turned to face him. "I don't understand."

"I don't know." His face fell, and he looked sullen. "I don't know. I only wanted to kill her…my mother. You knew her, you saw what she was like." He pulled his gun out of his shoulder holster and waved it around. "Well, I made her pay the price; she'll never belittle me again."

Fear wrapped around my heart and squeezed hard. "What did you do?"

"I killed her," he said, a satisfied smile crossing his face. "And I took my time, made her pay for everything she did to me."

His eyes seemed to go out of focus as he savored the kill. He was insane. I had to get away from him.

"Why didn't you kill her years ago? Why kill all those girls?" I shook my head. I didn't understand.

"There was something about them that reminded me of my mother. They couldn't be allowed to have children," he said, his jaw set.

"But Uncle Felix…" my voice trailed off.

"I feel really bad about that, Zoey. I really liked the old man. He didn't feel a thing. I did it as gently as I could. But, you see, I think he knew; he would have stopped me." The apologetic tone of his voice told me he was telling the truth. "Now you and Jax know too."

A chill ran down my spine. He took a step towards me and the impact of his words sunk in.

"If Jax knows, he'll hunt you down," I said, furtively looking around the room for something I could use as a weapon. I saw the coffee cups sitting on the counter but knew the brew would no longer be hot enough to throw it in his face.

"He already tried that. It didn't end well for him," he said.

"What did you do to him?" My heart sank.

Out of the corner of my eye I saw Karma on the kitchen counter behind Seth. She was in her zoom stance; the front part of her body hunched down and her back end in the air. She was almost ready for take-off.

His voice took on an ominous tone. "You'll find out soon enough."

Without warning, Karma launched herself and began darting around the kitchen at top speed. She leapt from the counter to the floor, to her cat tree, back up onto the counter, and then scrambled up Seth's back with all her claws out. He screamed in pain.

This was the chance I'd been looking for and I wasn't going to waste it. I grabbed one of the bar stools and hit Seth over the head with it, then bolted for the front door.

I heard him cursing loudly and out of the corner of my eye, I saw him pick up the stool and throw it against the wall.

When I reached the front door, I tried to open it, but the deadbolt was locked. The bastard had locked the door. With trembling fingers, I fumbled with the lock, but knew I was running out of time. The only chance I had was the window. I ran toward the large picture window in the living room, but I wasn't fast enough. Seth grabbed my hair and yanked me back into the living room. He whirled me around and slapped me so hard across the face I saw stars.

I fell to the floor, fighting for air.

I looked up at him. All I saw was a blood-thirsty animal who'd cornered its prey.

He stood and watched as I crawled across the floor and pulled myself up on the couch. The whole side of my face was screaming in pain, but I forced myself to concentrate.

He walked over to me and jerked me to my feet. He thrust my bag into my stomach. "Let's go. You're driving."

We walked out the front door, the muzzle of his gun in the middle of my back. He opened the car door for me, and I put my bag over my shoulder before getting into the car. "Don't even try it. I'll shoot you dead."

I had to half climb over the center console to the driver's seat. I started the car and screeched the tires as we drove down the street, hoping fervently that Jason would hear the noise and see what was happening.

"The Rockman house," he snarled. "You know where it is." I drove in silence and when we pulled down the driveway, I saw Jax's truck parked by the house.

Wordlessly I got out of the truck. Seth led me to the back window. He pointed his gun at me. "Get inside."

Obediently I climbed through the window and took my flashlight out of my bag. I turned around to face Seth who'd tucked his gun into the waistband of his jeans before starting to climb through the opening. As soon as he had one leg inside the house I reached up and grabbed the window sash, slamming it down on him as hard as I could.

He yelped in pain and I darted deeper into the house. I'd been here so many times now, I could practically find my way around in the dark.

I headed for the basement and turned on the flashlight so I wouldn't fall. I scrambled down the stairs. I could hear Seth limping across the floor above me.

I ran into the room that contained the shelves of ceramic molds, hid behind the shelf that was farthest away from the door and turned off my flashlight. As I crouched down in my hiding place, I could hear Seth coming down the basement stairs, and I was as quiet as I could possibly be.

"Zoey! I'm going to find you. There's no point in hiding," Seth said. In the light of his penlight, I saw him walk past the door of the room I was in.

"It looks like Zoey doesn't care about you as much as you thought she did," I heard him say to someone. He must have been talking to Jax.

Then I heard Jax yell out in pain. "You're only making it worse on Jax," Seth called out.

As much as I wanted to help Jax, I knew it wouldn't do anyone any good to come out of hiding. Jax was screaming in agony, and I had to put my fingers in my ears to block out most of the noise. I felt hot tears streaming down my face.

I couldn't just sit there and let Seth torture Jax. I had to do something. I grabbed one of the molds and ducked out of my hiding place just long enough to send it crashing into the wall on the opposite side of the room.

I heard Seth running down the hall towards me and peeked out to see where he was. "Zoey, I know you're in here." He was shining his penlight around the room.

As soon as he was directly in front of the shelves, I pushed on them with all the strength I had and sent them crashing down on top of him.

Cautiously, I approached him and turned on my flashlight. He wasn't moving, but his gun lay on the floor a few feet away from me.

In one swift motion, I grabbed the gun and ran out into the hallway toward the back room.

As I played my flashlight around the building, I saw Jax tied up, lying on a metal table.

"Jax!" I yelled and ran to him.

"Zoey," he said. His voice was weak.

I started to untie the ropes holding him down, but heard Seth swearing in the other room and the sound of broken ceramic molds being thrown around.

"Shh," I said to Jax and ran to the wall to hide in the shadows. I inched my way along the wall toward the door. I could hear Seth's footsteps coming down the hall.

As soon as he burst into the room, I hit him over the head as hard as I could with the butt end of the flashlight. He grabbed his head, and whirled around to face me, using the penlight to temporarily blind me.

I sidestepped the light and raised the gun, gripping it tightly in two hands like Jax had taught me. "Put your hands up and get on your knees!" I said.

Seth laughed. "You're just like all the others. You think you're in control of everything. You have been a pain in the ass ever since you showed up." He charged towards me and I pulled the trigger.

Seth grabbed his stomach. As he crumpled to the ground, he looked at me in disbelief. I dashed past him and rushed to Jax. I quickly untied the ropes and helped him sit up. I handed him the gun and my flashlight. "Shine it on Seth," I said.

I grabbed a long piece of rope and walked up to Seth. He was lying on the floor writhing in pain and hanging onto his stomach. His hands were covered in blood.

For a split second I felt sorry for him. I shook my head and wrapped the rope tight around his legs, knotting it several times.

"Let's get you out of here," I said to Jax. I noticed his pant leg was soaked in blood.

"Tell me what happened," I said, giving him a few moments to collect himself.

"I called Seth last night and told him to meet me here," he said, wincing in pain. "I confronted him, and we fought. I got shot in the leg."

I helped him get off the altar. He put an arm around my shoulders, and I wrapped an arm around his waist. "Lean on me."

We slowly made our way toward the door of the basement stairs. Halfway to the window, Jax had to rest, so he sat down on the floor.

I sat down next to him. "We've got to slow down this bleeding."

Jax took off his shirt and handed it to me. "Tie this around my leg just above the gun shot."

I did as he said, and it hurt my heart to see him in so much pain as I pulled the makeshift tourniquet tight. "Let's go."

In the distance I could hear sirens heading in our direction and by the time we got to my Jeep, Jason, a team of policemen, and first responders were waiting for us.

Jason rushed over to help me with Jax.

"It's Seth. He's in the basement," I said. I'd never been so happy to see anyone in my life.

Jason directed the policemen to the back of the house and came over to where I was standing.

"How did you find me?" I said, as we watched the EMTs treat Jax's wound.

"I tracked your phone. When I heard your tires screech, I knew something was wrong," he said and grimaced. "You going to yell at me again?"

"Not this time," I said, trying not to smile.

Jason put his arms around me and pulled me close. I wrapped my arms around his waist. "Let's go home," he whispered.

As we turned to leave, we were stopped by Captain Marino to follow him to the police station so I could give a statement. I agreed and told him about Seth bragging about killing his mother.

By the time I finished giving my statement it was almost midnight. Chief Marino assured me that Seth's mother was alive and well and when told about Seth saying he'd killed her, her response was, "He wouldn't have the guts."

As we walked up the stairs to my front porch, Jason took the keys out of my hand and opened the door. I was met by Karma who leapt into my arms and clung to me. Poor thing.

I tried to snuggle her, but she wriggled her way free, and jumped onto the kitchen counter to eat. Jason offered to stay, but I just wanted to be alone. I needed time to process everything.

After pouring myself a glass of wine, I went into my bedroom and got into bed, pulling the covers up to my chin. Karma curled up next to me and started to purr. It would be the first good night's sleep I'd had in many a moon.

EPILOGUE

3 MONTHS LATER

Seth recovered from his gunshot wound and sat in jail until his trial. He was facing two counts of kidnapping and first-degree murder charges for the deaths of Lisa Conrad and Lacey, as well as the stalking and attempted murder of myself and Jax. There wasn't enough evidence to charge him with the murders of the other two girls, although I was sure he'd killed them.

I'll never forget how he sat stoically at the defense table with his attorney. His eyes bored into me when I took the witness stand. I was so uncomfortable under his hateful gaze that it made reliving all the stalking and harassment incidents even harder.

Bea Perkins went to court with me, and I couldn't have gotten through it without her kindness and support. My mother, however, was nowhere to be found, and didn't even offer to be with me, nor did she give me any words of support or comfort. I should be used to her being that way by now, but it still hurt.

Seth's trial lasted over a week, and I barely slept the night the case was handed over to the jury. I was so scared there wasn't enough evidence against him, and he'd get a slap on the wrist because he used to be a cop.

I almost screamed in delight when the jury found him guilty on all counts and he was sentenced to two consecutive life sentences without the possibility of parole. He would also be extradited to face charges for the murder of the other three girls.

Jax recovered from the gunshot wound to his knee and was offered a promotion to take over Seth's job as a detective but turned it down for reasons I still don't quite understand. He left Hope Harbor two weeks ago. He moved back to Montana to take over his father's ranch. His father is getting too elderly to handle all the responsibilities by himself. Admirable for sure, but I know there's more to the story that he didn't want to share.

Bea Perkins is still working part time at St. Agatha's and playing mahjong with the Mavens of Mayhem. Atlas is spending more time at my house, and I have to admit I like having the big, goofy dog around. He gives me a sense of calm and safety.

Bea and I have dinner together at least twice a week, and have formed not only a deep friendship, but almost a mother-daughter relationship that I cherish.

Abby, my other next-door neighbor, moved out of Hope Harbor as well. Probably for the best. I confronted her about the money she still owed to my Uncle Felix, and the conversation turned ugly.

She told me the money was used to repair her car so she could get to and from work.

While I couldn't prove it, my suspicion was that she had a huge gambling problem and probably owed someone a lot of money.

I'd heard her talking to a friend of hers in Gil's recently about how she loved going to the casino.

A couple of days after she moved out and left for places unknown, two bouncer-type men showed up at her house. When they didn't get an answer, they came over to my house, and I told them that she'd moved out, but I didn't know where she'd gone.

Given their expressions, it was probably a good thing that she disappeared by her own accord, and not because she was involved with the type of people that could cause her to disappear against her will.

Jason bought the Rockman house from the city of Hope Harbor and has started to restore it to its former glory. As much as I want to go out there to see what progress has been made, I just haven't been able to force myself to cross the threshold since the altercation with Seth.

He's taken pictures of the work he's done and proudly shows them to me every week. He also told me there're boxes full of stuff up in the attic that he hasn't had time to go through yet, as well as old furniture pieces he's going to restore.

When he has time, he's going to put them in his truck and bring them to my house so I can go through them at my leisure. His excuse is that he doesn't have the time to go through them because many of the boxes have old photographs, documents, and other items that he said, "would be better left up to you to organize."

Maybe it's just his way of keeping me in his life and wanting me to be as excited about the house as he is. The truth is, I'm anxious to dig into the boxes and see what secrets they hold about the Rockman family. Ever since I found that book in the closet of one of the bedrooms with all the potions and other information, I've become obsessed with the Rockman family. The Hope Harbor

Historical Society has already applied for another grant so I can continue my work on the witch cemetery and the Rockman's.

Jason and I are taking our budding relationship slowly. Actually... it's at a snail's pace because of our jobs and the house restoration, but we do go out to dinner every Saturday night to catch up. Lately he's been getting clingy and controlling. Definitely a turn off.

As for me, I'm still working with my clients, although the work for the FBI has increased and keeps me extremely busy. I've also made an effort to become more social by attending town festivals and other events.

Karma, my adorable kitten, is now almost a full-grown cat and as sassy as ever. Jason teases me that I'm going to turn into a crazy cat lady because of how spoiled she is, but I don't care. What's the point of having a cat or other animal and not spoiling it silly? In fact, I'm thinking of getting another cat to keep Karma company.

COMING SOON

CayellePublishing.com

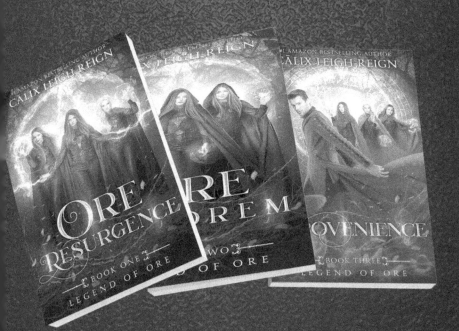

amazon.com

SHOP BOOKS
CayellePublishing.com

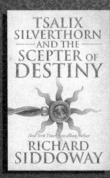

amazon.com

CPSIA information can be obtained
at www.ICGtesting.com
Printed in the USA
LVHW111524151220
674002LV00009B/160